THE OWL AND THE PUSSYCAT

THE OWL AND

THE PUSSYCAT

BY BILL MANHOFF

1965
DOUBLEDAY & COMPANY, INC.
GARDEN CITY, NEW YORK

All of the characters in this book
are fictitious, and any resemblance
to actual persons, living or dead,
is purely coincidental.

Photographs by courtesy of Friedman-Abeles

For Joy

In Gratitude

THE OWL AND THE PUSSYCAT was first presented by Philip Rose, Pat Fowler, and Seven Arts Productions at the Anta Theatre, New York City, on November 18, 1964, with the following cast:

F. Sherman	Alan Alda
Doris W.	Diana Sands

Directed by Arthur Storch

Settings and lighting by Jo Mielziner

Costumes by Florence Klotz

Act One

Act Two

Act Three

ACT ONE

Scene 1

Felix Sherman's apartment in San Francisco. A third floor walk-up with a partly obstructed view of the Golden Gate Bridge through a large leaded window. It is the room of a self-advertising intellectual—indifferently furnished in a purely functional, almost Spartan way. There's a fireplace—a closet door and doors leading to the bedroom and bathroom on the right—a door to the hall on the left . . . a portable type-writer on a small table at the window, an open dictionary, etc. Slightly at odds with the informality of the furnishings is the precise formality of their arrangement—chairs are lined up—books precisely arranged. A dedicated orderliness has done its best with discouraging material.

At rise the only light comes through the window from the moon. There is an insistent knocking at the door, stage right. There is no response.

DORIS (*off stage*). Mr. Sherman! . . . Mr. Sherman! . . . (etc., etc.)

(*Through the door from the bedroom comes* FELIX SHER-MAN. *He's tying the belt of a robe he has slipped on over his pajamas. He's in his late twenties. He turns on a lamp and goes toward the door.*)

[3]

FELIX. Yes? Who is it?

DORIS (*off stage*). Mr. Sherman?

FELIX. Who's there?

DORIS (*off stage*). I have to see you, Mr. Sherman.

(*Somewhat reassured at finding the caller is female,* FELIX *goes closer to the door.*)

FELIX. Who are you—what is it?

DORIS (*off stage*). You don't know me, but it's terribly important.

FELIX. It's very late. I never open the door to strangers at this hour.

DORIS (*off stage*). I'll only be a minute—please—please, it's a matter of life and death.

FELIX. Are you alone?

DORIS (*off stage*). Yes, I am. I'm just a little girl and I'm all alone, and I need your help.

(FELIX *goes to the door.*)

FELIX. What's it about? Is anybody chasing you?

DORIS (*off stage*). No, no, I just can't discuss it through the door—it's extremely personal. Please— I beg you.

FELIX. Swear to me that you're alone.

DORIS (*off stage*). What did you say? Swear to you?

FELIX. Say "As God is my judge, I am all alone."

DORIS (*off stage*). As God is my judge, I am only a little girl all alone here in the hall—and I'm not running away from anybody.

(*Obviously with great misgivings,* FELIX *opens the door.* DORIS WAVERLY *enters. She is twenty-six—hard—alert— protected at every human point by a thick shell and physically sturdier than* FELIX. *As soon as* FELIX *sees her he tries to close the door, but she forces her way past him.* FELIX *retreats in nervous confusion.* DORIS *follows him.*)

Hello, Pansy—rat fink pansy!

FELIX. You lied about your size!

DORIS. You spider—you cockroach!

FELIX. You're making a mistake. I'm afraid you have the wrong apartment.

DORIS. I just wanted to get a look at you.

[5]

FELIX. It's a mistake!

DORIS. Oh will you listen to her! Mistake! You didn't spy on me from your window and call my landlord, huh?

FELIX. I don't know you.

DORIS. Well, I should have known! Any queer who peeps at girls through his window like a dirty weasel wouldn't be man enough to admit it.

FELIX. You gained entry here under false pretenses . . . You have no right . . .

DORIS. Was it fun? Did you wish you could do what the big boys were doing?

FELIX. I have no idea what you're talking about.

DORIS. "I have no idea what you're talking about." Come on, don't give me that! He told me. You're the one that called all right. "Sherman."

FELIX. If you leave immediately—I won't call the police—

DORIS. Call them. You said you would. You told Gould you were gonna call the police . . . you know you told him that, you slimy snail—you bedbug . . . you cockroach.

FELIX. I advise you to curb your foul mouth and stop making obscenities out of God's harmless little creatures.

[6]

DORIS. Why don't you curb your foul rotten mind. Try to be a man for once.

FELIX. Now listen to me—

DORIS. You're lucky I'm too refined to beat you up—the way I feel—

FELIX. Will you listen to me . . . you're insane!

DORIS. You're lucky I can't stand physical violence.

FELIX. Now look—something has happened to you obviously—

DORIS (*starting to get weepy*). What has happened is that I have been thrown out of my room. At two o'clock in the morning.

FELIX. He did that? That was unnecessary.

DORIS. Then you admit it. You called Gould, right?

FELIX. I don't have to admit anything.

DORIS (*going to window*). I don't know how you even saw anything this far away. You must have eyes like a vulture. Why did you pick on me? (*The flood of anger is running out—leaving her weak.*) How dare you do something like this? I get sick when I think there are people like you! I took money from a couple of gentlemen—did that hurt you?

[7]

FELIX (*condescending*). You must expect a certain number of people to respect the laws. That's what holds society together.

DORIS. Three cheers for you! And I'm not society, huh? I don't have to get held together?

FELIX. My dear woman, you were breaking the law. If you find yourself in trouble it is only . . .

DORIS (*notices a pair of field glasses and picks them up*). So this is how you saw! Oh now, it's bad enough with the naked eye—but with spyglasses—now that is just plain dirty, mister. I'm sorry! When you work at it this hard—filthy, mister! Filthy, filthy!

FELIX (*defensive*). I'm a writer. A writer is an observer. I have a right to those.

DORIS. You want me to tell you what you're full of?

FELIX. I wouldn't expect you to understand.

DORIS. You are nothing but a dirty, filthy Peeping Tom!

FELIX. Why don't you ever pull down your window shade?

DORIS. I never pull down my window shade. I hate window shades.

FELIX. That's your privilege, by all means.

[8]

DORIS. I keep forgetting the world is full of finks. That's my trouble. I ought to get it tattooed on the back of my hand—"Watch out for Finks."

(*Annoyed,* FELIX *suddenly sits at the typewriter and types rapidly on a white card, which he then pins to the bulletin board.*)

What are you doing? (*Reading it.*) "A rule worth making is worth keeping." What is that?

FELIX. That's to remind me never to open my door after midnight.

DORIS. Why don't you make one to remind you to stop being a fink?

FELIX. I wish you would stop using that ugly word.

DORIS. You don't like it? Too bad! Fink. Pansy fink, queer fink, Peeping Tom fink, fink fink, you fink!

FELIX. Feel better? (*He goes to the door and opens it.*) If you're sure your poison sacs are empty you can go.

DORIS. Just tell me where I'm supposed to go?

FELIX. Don't you have a friend you could stay with?

DORIS. Not that I can move in on at two A.M.

FELIX. How about a hotel?

DORIS. I got seventy-two cents. The son of a bitch took all of my money.

FELIX. Who did?

DORIS. Barney Gould, the landlord.

FELIX. How could he do that?

DORIS. While he was helping you hold society together with one hand—he was robbing me with the other. He said you saw me take money from a couple of—and you were gonna call the cops and if I gave him the money he'd cover up with the cops—that's how could he!

FELIX. He was lying to you. All I did was ask him if he knew what was going on in his building.

DORIS. Gee, that was big of you!

FELIX. Well, I felt he should know. For his own protection.

DORIS. Oh sweet! You're just a big mother, aren't you? Now will you lend me five bucks so I can get a room? I'll pay you back.

FELIX. I don't have any money. I got paid today and haven't cashed my check.

[10]

DORIS. I never knew a fink that did have any money.

FELIX. Don't you know anybody you could call?

(DORIS *has fallen onto a chair. She's defeated and near tears.*)

Don't you have any family? (*Looking at the couch.*) You can't stay here!

DORIS. I'd rather sleep in the gutter.

FELIX. It's a matter of taste, I suppose.

(*On her last line,* DORIS *has gone to the door. She brings in a large suitcase, a portable TV set, and a radio.*)

What are you doing?

DORIS. Get me a sheet and a blanket for that couch.

FELIX. You're not staying here. Oh, no—no!

DORIS. Naturally I'm staying. Where have I got to go?

FELIX. I thought you were looking forward to a night in the gutter.

DORIS. Just get a blanket, will you please . . . and stop being so goddam bitchy! Come on, come on.

FELIX. Very well, you may stay the night.

DORIS. Thanks for nothing.

(FELIX *starts to answer. Changes his mind. Goes to the bedroom.* DORIS *takes off her coat—tosses it carelessly onto the coffee table, sets the suitcase on the sofa and opens it—she takes a nightgown out of the suitcase and closes it.* FELIX *comes from the bedroom with one folded sheet, a blanket, and dumps the sheet and blanket on the sofa. He glares at her.* DORIS *plugs in the television set.*)

What kind of reception do you get?

FELIX. I wouldn't know. I've never had a television set.

DORIS. Oh, that's right—you got your spyglasses! By the way, how was I on the late, late show?

(FELIX *goes to the coffeepot and pours coffee into a plastic cup.*)

FELIX. You're not planning to watch television at this hour?

DORIS (*tucking sheet under sofa cushion*). It's the only way I can get to sleep—I won't play it loud. Listen— I don't want to be here—if you had kept your mouth shut . . .

FELIX. And if you had kept your window shade down . . .

[12]

DORIS. You got a sweetheart in there? Some bouncy young boy or do you dig the rough trade—

FELIX. You're an alley cat, aren't you? On your back and rip out their guts with your hind claws.

DORIS. And what do you do, lover? Pull their hair and scratch out their eyes? Give me some of that coffee . . . please.

(FELIX *starts to pour a cup for her.*)

No. A whole cup'll keep me awake. Just give me a sip of yours. Do you ever write for television?

FELIX. No thank you.

(FELIX *crosses to her and she takes his cup—takes two sips, watching him.*)

DORIS. What kind of a writer are you? Did I ever hear of you?

FELIX. No.

DORIS. Did anybody?

FELIX. Voices like mine are drowned out by the clatter of the cash register. That's *two* sips—

(DORIS *gives him back the cup.* FELIX *starts to drink— switches the cup and drinks from the other side.*)

[13]

DORIS. Now, what was that you just did?

FELIX. What?

DORIS. Drinking out of the other side like that—

FELIX. Oh—I always do that—it's a reflex—

DORIS. Yeah—sure it is.

FELIX. Really—I'm a hypochondriac.

DORIS. You make me feel like I'm a cockroach and I just crawled into your clean little house and you're trying to get up the nerve to squash me—that's the way you make me feel.

FELIX. Oh my God, you're crazy!

DORIS. Listen, mister—I don't want to see that in your eyes when you look at me—I am a model. I have been in many television commercials at a time when I weighed 105, which unfortunately I don't any more. So don't you dare turn that cup around, you hear? You don't catch anything from a model—do you hear me—I may turn a trick or two, but *I am a model!*

(DORIS's *voice has risen hysterically. At this point there's a knock at the wall.*)

[14]

FELIX. Listen—you can't stay here. Why don't you try the YWCA?

DORIS. With seventy-two cents? That Christian the YWCA is not—

FELIX. Will you try to be quiet—there's an old man next door.

DORIS. And you don't want him to think you switched to girls, right?

FELIX. Now look—

DORIS (*interrupting, as she exits to bathroom*). Don't worry about it—just leave me alone. I'll try to get out of here before you wake up.

(*He starts to bedroom.*)

(*Off stage.*) Do me a favor—if you wake up and I'm still here, yell before you come out so I can close my eyes. I don't wanna have to look at you first thing in the morning. Where's the john? Excuse me—the jane? . . . the bawth-room!

FELIX. It's in there. Good night.

DORIS (*off stage*). Good night, fink.

(FELIX *exits to the bedroom.*)

[15]

(*We hear the soundtrack of the TV movie clearly now.*)

OLD WOMAN'S VOICE. Then you knew—all the time.

OLD MAN'S VOICE. Yes—I knew he was guilty.

OLD WOMAN'S VOICE. Then why, Ben?

OLD MAN'S VOICE. Why did I let them convict me for his crime?

OLD WOMAN'S VOICE. Thirty years—thirty long years . . . Why, Ben? Why?

(DORIS *enters from the bathroom, wearing her nightgown— she watches the movie for a couple of lines of dialogue.*)

OLD WOMAN'S VOICE. You had so much to live for—the governorship. There were those who thought you had a chance for the White House.

OLD MAN'S VOICE. Yes—there were those who said that . . .

OLD WOMAN'S VOICE. And you threw it all away, Ben, to save him. Why? He was a thief and a drunkard.

OLD MAN'S VOICE. Why? Because a girl with cornflower blue eyes and yellow hair loved him.

OLD WOMAN'S VOICE. Oh Ben, my eyes are still cornflower blue, but my hair is all white now.

OLD MAN'S VOICE. Not to me—Alice—to me it'll always be yellow.

OLD WOMAN'S VOICE. Ben—you mean—oh no!

OLD MAN'S VOICE. Then they didn't tell you? Yes, Alice—I'm blind, an accident in the prison library.

OLD WOMAN'S VOICE. No, you're not blind, Ben, for as long as I live, you have two cornflower blue eyes—

OLD MAN'S VOICE. Alice—

OLD WOMAN'S VOICE. Oh Ben—

(*And the music comes up for a big finish.* DORIS *crosses to the set.*)

ANNOUNCER. And that concludes the late, late show—well—

(*The voice is killed as* DORIS *turns off the set. She turns on the radio—it doesn't work—she shakes it—desperately.*)

DORIS (*shouts*). God damn it! Hey fink, fink!

(FELIX *enters.*)

FELIX. Now what?

DORIS. My radio won't work. I must have banged it, coming up the stairs!

[17]

FELIX. Do you really have to—

DORIS. It's the only way I can go to sleep. You got a radio?

FELIX. No.

DORIS. What'll I do now? Why did I have to come up here?

FELIX. Why not correct your mistake? Leave!

DORIS. I should have just given a certain friend of mine a dollar
to beat you up.

FELIX. A dollar? Can't be much of a beating.

DORIS. He's a friend. He would do it for nothing, but I make
him take a dollar.

FELIX. I see.

DORIS. What's so goddam funny? I'll send him around tomorrow. I guarantee you won't think it's so funny. Now I'll
never get to sleep.

FELIX. Why can't you sleep?

DORIS. I'm very high-strung.

FELIX. I don't have any sleeping pills or I'd—

[18]

DORIS. I don't take sleeping pills. I never take them. They're enervating.

FELIX. How about a hot bath—that'll relax you.

DORIS (*talking in a compulsive rush*). I never take baths. They're enervating too. You know that word—"enervating"? Most people think it means just the opposite of what it really means.

(FELIX *walks back toward the bedroom in the middle of her speech, yawning—yearning for sleep.* DORIS *raises her voice to a shout.* FELIX *stops.*)

Another word that kills me is naïve—I always thought it was "nave" you know. How do you pronounce it?

FELIX. I never use it.

DORIS. I mean I heard the word na'ive but—

(THE NEIGHBOR *knocks.*)

FELIX. What's the matter with you? What are you trying to do? I got up at five-thirty this morning.

DORIS. Listen, I know this sounds crazy, but will you sit here for a little while and talk to me?

FELIX. You act as though you were afraid to be alone.

[19]

DORIS. I usually fall asleep with the television on or the radio
—but now my radio's on the fritz and it's too late for TV.

FELIX. It's too late for me, too. I'm signing off. (*Sings.*) Oh
say can you see by the dawn's early light— This is Channel
Sherman signing off for the night.

DORIS (*laughs much too hard*). That's pretty funny. I never
would have thought you had a sense of humor.

FELIX. I'm a funny fink.

DORIS. Just goes to show you never can tell about people.

(*As she talks* FELIX *turns and makes another try for the
bedroom—without a pause and without changing her tone
or her volume,* DORIS *goes on.*)

If you take one more step I'm gonna scream at the top of
my lungs.

FELIX. For God's sake—

DORIS. I can't help it. Do you think I can help it? I can't fall
asleep unless I'm listening to something. Read me something—you got any magazines?

FELIX. Isn't there any other way for you to get to sleep?

DORIS. There's only one other way.

THE OWL AND THE PUSSYCAT

FELIX. That wouldn't interest me.

DORIS. That is not what I meant—evil-minded!

FELIX. Listen—I must get some sleep.

DORIS. So must I—which I would if not for some dirty rotten bastard who you and I both know. Pardon my language.

FELIX (*humoring a child*). All right—all right. What do you want?

DORIS. Read to me. Read me anything and I'll fall asleep. Nothing with big words. I hate big words.

(FELIX *looks around the room—looks at* DORIS—*looks at his books—looks back at* DORIS—*obviously decides he has nothing suitable.*)

Well?

FELIX. We're out of bedtime stories. What was the other way you have of falling asleep?

DORIS. Huh? Oh—that's only in the winter when it's real cold— I huddle myself down in bed under about a million blankets—it's a wonder I don't suffocate . . . Come on read to me—anything.

(FELIX *picks up a small bronze bust—for a second considers hitting her with it.*)

FELIX. I could put you to sleep with Shakespeare.

DORIS. Shakespeare gives me a headache.

FELIX. I don't have anything you'd like. I don't have any comic books, movie magazines, or any other literature of that nature!

DORIS (*yawning*). Don't stop—your voice is very enervating. You know what that means? Oh yeah—I told you before. Come on—keep talking—

FELIX (*looks about desperately—picks up box of breakfast food —reads the label*). Ingredients: oat flour, wheat starch, sugar, salt, cinnamon, sodium phosphate, calcium carbonate, artificial coloring, iron, niacin, thiamine and riboflavin, caramel, vegetable oil with freshness preserved by butylated hydroxylene and—

DORIS. No—that's no good—I'm getting hungry. Hey—read me one of your stories. Read me your latest one.

FELIX. You wouldn't like it. (*Remembering.*) Fourscore and seven years ago our fathers brought forth on this continent a new nation, conceived in liberty and dedicated to the proposition that all men are created equal—equal . . . (*Stops—stuck. He sits on the end of the sofa, exhausted.*)

DORIS. Don't stop—that's nice—the Declaration of Independence—right?

FELIX. No. Custer's farewell address to the Indians.

DORIS. Oh yes—that's right—why'd you stop?

FELIX. I don't remember any more. Listen—I'm exhausted—

DORIS. Why wouldn't I like your story?

FELIX. It has no rape scene, no beautiful people, and no happy ending.

DORIS. Let's hear it. Maybe I can spot where you went wrong.

FELIX. You ought to be ashamed of yourself! A big girl like you afraid to be alone . . . (*He yawns.*)

DORIS. Isn't that ridiculous! Ever since I was a kid—I tell you it's not being alone that's scary—I wouldn't mind being alone—but there's somebody there—I can hear him breathing—he just stands there breathing and it just panics me—I had this analysis, you know, for six months and the doctor told me . . . (*Stops.*) Hey—

(*He's dozed off.*)

FELIX. Oh— What were you saying?

DORIS. About being alone—my analyst said—

FELIX. You were analyzed?

[23]

DORIS. Of course.

FELIX. Really?

DORIS. There's a brain in there—honest!

FELIX. What kind of a doctor?

DORIS. Jewish.

FELIX. No. I mean—never mind. What did he say?

DORIS. Oh, I hate that!

FELIX. What?

DORIS. "Never mind." Like "forget it, you're too dumb to understand."

FELIX. Oh no—it was just a foolish question on my part.

DORIS. Really?

FELIX. Sure. That's why I said "never mind." What did he tell you?

DORIS. He said I was afraid to be alone because of unconscious guilt.

FELIX. Guilt is very bad.

DORIS. It's enervating.

FELIX. If you don't let me go to sleep you're gonna be completely enervated by guilt feelings tomorrow.

DORIS. Never mind, wise guy! Read me your story.

FELIX (*picks up typewritten script*). You won't like it.

DORIS. If it puts me to sleep I'll love it.

FELIX (*reading*). Scream . . .

DORIS. "Scream." That's the title, right? "Scream."

FELIX. Yes.

DORIS. That's a wild title.

FELIX. Thank you. (*Reads.*) The sun spit morning into Werner's face—one eyelid fluttered—dragging the soul back screaming from its stealthy flight to death—

DORIS (*sitting up*). The sun spit morning into this guy's face?

FELIX. Yes.

DORIS. You were right.

FELIX. When?

DORIS. I don't like it. I hate it.

FELIX. It wasn't written for you to like.

DORIS. Why wasn't it written for me to like? I'm the public—

FELIX. You're raising your voice.

DORIS. The sun spit morning into his face!

FELIX. Shh! What are you getting angry about?

DORIS. What right do you have to put down a terrible thing like that in a story—"The sun spit morning in a man's face."

FELIX. All right—you don't like it—but calm down.

DORIS. Yeah—look at me! I always get mad at stuff like that.

FELIX. Just because you don't understand it?

DORIS. It makes me feel shut out—you know? It makes me mad as hell! You know once I threw a clock at the TV.

FELIX. Really?

DORIS. I swear to God. It was Maurice Evans in something— poetry—I don't know—and all of a sudden—bam—sixty-three bucks for a new tube.

FELIX. And with just the turn of a knob you could have had the reassurance of mediocrity.

DORIS. Damn it, are you talking to me or not?

FELIX. Why do you get so angry at anything that's over your head?

DORIS. I can't help it. When I was going to this headshrinker —every once in a while he'd start talking big words and I'd get so boiling mad! Once I put my dress on inside out—

FELIX. You took psychiatric sessions with your dress off?

DORIS. Oh hell—why did I let that slip out! (*Hiccups.*)

FELIX. It's perfectly all right. The barter system is time-honored.

DORIS (*getting angry*). Now I don't know what that means either, mister—

FELIX. Take it easy now—

DORIS. You know what you are? You're inflabious. (*Hic.*)

FELIX. Inflabious?

DORIS. Yeah.

FELIX. What does that mean?

[27]

DORIS (*thumbing her nose*). Ah ha! How does it feel? I'm not gonna tell you!

FELIX. You just made up a word?

DORIS. How do I know you're not making up yours?

FELIX. Mine are in the dictionary.

DORIS. That's *your* story!

FELIX. I suppose it never occurred to you that as an alternative to getting angry you might make some attempt to understand whatever it is that confuses you?

DORIS. Why? Why should I? What about people making some attempt to not confuse me? (*Hic.*)

FELIX. Because progress does not lie in the pampering of the brainless.

DORIS. Drop (*hic*) dead! Damn it!

FELIX. Hold your breath.

DORIS. Hold yours . . .

FELIX. Maybe you can hiccup yourself to sleep.

DORIS. You better not be so damn funny—people have been known to (*hic*) die from the hiccups.

FELIX. Drink a glass of water.

DORIS. That never works with me. Only one thing works with me—you gotta scare me.

FELIX. How the devil am I gonna scare a holy terror like you?

DORIS (*hic*). I get them very deep—it's a strain on the heart, so stop fooling around and scare me (*hic*) or I'll scream.

(FELIX *turns and walks around the sofa—suddenly pounces with clawed hands, snarling like a tiger.*)

Oh come (*hic*) on!

(FELIX *drops down behind sofa—*DORIS *hiccups twice.* FELIX *suddenly appears on all fours around the end of the sofa, rising menacingly and hissing like a snake.*)

It's no use. I was expecting it. You have to do it when I'm not (*hic*) expecting it.

FELIX. Oh that's ridiculous! How can I do that—you're waiting for me to frighten you.

DORIS. Well make me (*hic*) forget about it—stupid. Then when my mind is on (*hic*) something else—then do it!

FELIX. When your mind is on something else!

[29]

DORIS. Of course stupid! Change the subject—put me off my (*hic*) guard.

FELIX. Some weather we're having. It's a wonderful summer, isn't it?

DORIS. Beautiful (*hic*).

FELIX. I think it's quite a bit warmer than it was last year at this time. Don't you?

DORIS. I was in Chicago (*hic*) last summer.

FELIX. That's an interesting city, Chicago.

DORIS. I didn't (*hic*) like it. Come on will you—you want me to hiccup to death? (*Hic.*)

FELIX. I'm putting you off your guard!

DORIS. I'm off my (*hic*) guard by now. Stupid!

FELIX. You're expecting it now.

DORIS. I am not (*hic*). Come on, will you!

(FELIX *gives a hideous roar.* DORIS *looks at* FELIX *for a second, then:*)

You're right. I was (*hic*) expecting it.

FELIX. Listen—I'm through—I'm finished—I'm exhausted. I'm going to bed—I don't care what you do—you can scream yourself sick—I just don't care!

(FELIX *exits to bedroom.* DORIS *turns, facing audience.*)

DORIS. Dirty son of (*hic*) bitch! Cockroach!

(*Behind her,* FELIX *creeps on tiptoe from the bedroom.*)

Rotten (*hic*) pervert. I could die for all he cares. (*Hic.*) I could die right—

(*At this point, unheard by her,* FELIX *is right behind* DORIS. *Suddenly he growls and puts his hands around her neck.* DORIS *jumps in terror. She turns and clouts* FELIX *in the face.*)

FELIX. What's the idea!

DORIS. You wanna give somebody a heart attack? You maniac, you wanna kill me?

FELIX (*nursing his face*). You're out of your mind!

DORIS. Do you know how dangerous that is—to scare some-body like that. My heart is pounding like crazy.

FELIX. You asked me to scare you—

[31]

DORIS. I didn't ask for a heart attack. I'm fainting! Do you have any vodka?

FELIX. No—all I have is a little cooking sherry. What you need now is sleep—I'll leave you alone so you can drop off.

DORIS. Cooking sherry! You know, you're not real.

FELIX. Wait a minute. I think I have a little scotch.

DORIS. That's better.

FELIX (*looking in cupboard*). Unless I gave it away—

(THE NEIGHBOR *knocks and shouts "Quiet down!"*)

no here it is. (*He takes out a bottle with about two inches of liquor—pours her a drink.*)

DORIS. That's good—hurry up—will you—

(FELIX *hands her the glass. She drinks.*)

Ugh—what is it—cooking scotch?

FELIX. Someone left it here. Your hiccups are gone.

DORIS. My whole insides are gone.

FELIX. Now how about going to sleep. I can't stand up any more . . . Good night. (*He starts toward bedroom.*)

[32]

DORIS (*screams*). Don't you leave me alone!

(*There's one knock on wall, then—*)

THE NEIGHBOR. Quiet down or I'll call the police.

FELIX (*yells*). Call them! It's a good idea!

DORIS. Shh! Not so loud.

FELIX (*still yelling*). I'm the one who should be calling the police. I'm an idiot.

DORIS. Stop yelling.

FELIX. Tyrannized in my own home by an ignorant whore! What's the matter with me?

DORIS (*angry—but starting to cry*). You were just being nice to an unfortunate person because it's your fault she's unfortunate.

FELIX. No—I've been on the defensive—I've actually been apologetic because I did my duty as a citizen.

DORIS (*shouting through her tears*). All right, citizen—shoot me, citizen! Call the cops, citizen! Save America, citizen!

FELIX (*shouting*). It's not my fault you're a whore.

DORIS. Stop calling me that! I'm a model, and an actress.

[33]

FELIX. You're not what you call yourself, you're what you are!

DORIS. Will you stop yelling—he'll call the cops.

FELIX (*still yelling*). He can't. He doesn't have a phone.

DORIS. Well, stop yelling. A gentleman doesn't yell at a lady.

FELIX (*sarcastic*). Excuse me, lady—

DORIS. Listen, you—you don't know anything about me. You have no right to even talk to me—because you don't even know who I am! So what right have you got? Do you know that I never take a trick to whom I have not been properly introduced? You can't just pick me up on the street—

FELIX (*sarcastic*). Pardon me—is that so?

DORIS. You bet your ass that's so! I may be a prostitute—but I am not promiscuous!

FELIX. Oh, what a nice distinction!

DORIS. You bet it is! Did you know I was in two TV commercials? A Razzle Laundry Soap and a Platzburg Beer? No! You don't know anything about me. Nothing! But you sound off your big mouth!

FELIX. Look—I've got a couple of dollars—maybe you can get a room down on Van Ness.

DORIS. Call the cops—

FELIX. Look—I'm exhausted.

DORIS. Call the cops—I want you to—I don't care any more.

FELIX. I don't want to call the police. Look, Doris.

DORIS. Who told you my name is Doris?

FELIX. It's on your nightgown.

DORIS. Who gave you permission to read my nightgown? (*Turning away from him.*) Don't call me "Doris"—you don't know who I am. Don't talk to me.

FELIX. All right—Miss—whoever you are—your staying here is no good for either one of us.

DORIS (*quiet now*). Nobody knows who I am. Wouldn't it be funny if I didn't know who I was either?

FELIX. All you need is some sleep. You'll feel better.

DORIS. Oh, I feel better—I'm okay—(*she sighs deeply and shudders*).

FELIX (*sudden attack of guilt*). Listen—I want you to know I'm really sorry I did what I did—I mean telling your landlord.

[35]

DORIS. Forget it. Maybe it's for the best—it was time I got out of that crummy room. Anyway, I've had it with Frisco. I think I'll move to L.A. and change my name. Maybe I can get a job—I know a guy in an advertising agency in L.A.

FELIX. Can you do secretarial work?

DORIS. I can't spell. I'm so dumb—

FELIX. You're not dumb at all.

DORIS. Who's not dumb, me? You really mean that? I know you do, otherwise you would never say it, right?

FELIX. That's right.

DORIS. You're the type. I feel dumb though.

FELIX. You just don't think. You live almost exclusively in the atmosphere of your emotions, reacting to everything emotionally—don't you?

DORIS. I guess so. Like getting so mad when I don't understand something—right?

FELIX. Right.

DORIS. Could a person get over something like that?

FELIX. I would say there's a lot more hope for you than there

[36]

would be for a girl who was left completely unmoved by what she didn't understand.

DORIS. You know you talk great, you really do.

FELIX. Language is my business.

DORIS. You make any money at it?

FELIX. I don't write to make money.

DORIS. You'd take money if they gave it to you, naturally, right?

FELIX. If they gave it to me for writing my way. The trouble is they only give you money for writing their way.

DORIS. Yeah, well I guess they figure it's their money.

FELIX. I think that's the way they figure, yes.

DORIS. Go argue with that! Anyway, you sure do know a lot of words!

FELIX. You like words, don't you?

DORIS. When I understand them.

FELIX. You should stop running away from your mind. It won't bite you.

DORIS. Is that what I'm doing?

FELIX. Most of the world is. Fleeing the pain of thought.

DORIS (*reverently*). "Fleeing the pain of thought." Did you make that up?

FELIX. It's from a poem I wrote.

DORIS (*savoring it*). "Fleeing the pain of thought." (*She suddenly turns her head—puts a handkerchief to her face.*) You wanna make love to me?

FELIX. No, I don't.

DORIS (*sudden rush of embarrassment*). Oh my God!

FELIX. What?

DORIS. Nothing. I just thought of how I came in here before, screaming such terrible language.

FELIX. You were pretty angry.

DORIS. I'm so ashamed. I know you'll never believe it but when I'm not mad, I'm very refined.

FELIX. I believe it. I think you have to be very tough because you're very soft.

[38]

DORIS. Gee, that's nice. Thank you. It doesn't make sense. But thank you.

FELIX. You're welcome. It makes sense.

DORIS. Anyway, I have this horrible temper. It makes me into a completely different person.

FELIX. I'm sorry I told your landlord. I really am. It was an act of self-righteousness. I don't often do things like that.

DORIS. Oh listen—what the hell. (*Correcting herself immediately.*) What the devil. You had a strong feeling that it was the right thing to do—so you did it. You can't help those things.

FELIX. You're very gracious.

DORIS. I am, really? Gracious?

FELIX. Yes.

DORIS. You know I once wrote an essay in High School and the teacher thought it was so good she made me read it to the class. The subject was How I FEEL MOTION PICTURES AND TELEVISION HAVE AFFECTED MY LIFE. She sent it to a couple of magazines, but they sent it back.

FELIX. I know the feeling.

DORIS. *Reader's Digest* and some other one. I never should

[39]

have left school—only my mother got sick and my father started drinking again and my goddam brother (pardon the language) joined the Navy, and to tell you the truth, I figured what did an actress need with a high school diploma anyway, and this agent felt he could get me into this semi-professional theatre group, which never got off the ground, as it turned out. I had two copies of the essay, but I lost them both.

FELIX. What essay?—oh yes—

DORIS. How I Feel Motion Pictures and Television Have Affected My Life. I thought I would write it out again, but I can't remember it. Let me ask you something— Are there books you can read that will increase your intelligence?

FELIX. Not really.

DORIS. That was a stupid question, wasn't it?

FELIX. No.

DORIS. Then what are you smiling at?

FELIX. I don't know.

(DORIS *leans forward suddenly and kisses* FELIX *on the lips.*)

FELIX (*after a frozen beat*). Reading books can only add to your information.

[40]

DORIS. I have always felt it was really like a sickness, being you know—queer. It's certainly nothing to be ashamed of or looked down on. (Like my goddam brother loves to beat them up.) Did you have a bad experience with a girl? Is that what did it?

FELIX. What makes you so sure I'm queer? Isn't it possible I'm just not interested?

DORIS. You mean I'm not your type?

FELIX. I don't mean that—

DORIS. Do you think I'm pretty?

FELIX. Yes, I do.

DORIS. I'm not really. I just make you think I am.

FELIX. How do you do that?

DORIS. It's just a trick. You just gotta act pretty—it's hard to explain.

FELIX. In other words, you're not pretty—you're just a good actress.

DORIS. Well, I'm not a dog—but, well—yeah, I never thought about it—but it is—it's acting—watch—now I look pretty —right?

FELIX. Uh huh.

DORIS. Okay—now watch—(DORIS *lets her face and body slump into vacant stupidity.*)

FELIX. That's amazing! Like two different girls!

DORIS. *Now* you're putting me on!

FELIX. No—I'm not!

DORIS. It's hard to tell with you . . . anyway—what's your name?

FELIX. Sherman.

DORIS. I know that from the doorbell. F. Sherman. What does the F. stand for?

FELIX. "Fink."

DORIS. Come on!

FELIX. Felix.

DORIS. "Felix." Ugh! It sounds like stepping on snails.

FELIX. What's your name?

DORIS. Doris.

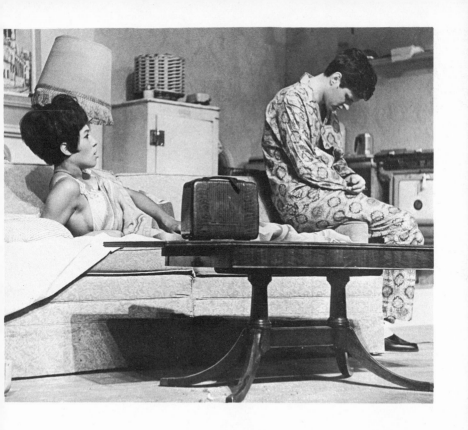

FELIX. Doris what?

DORIS. I don't know. I'm between names right now. I've been using "Waverly," but it's been bad luck. I gotta change it —you know I got a feeling I've seen you some place.

FELIX. At the bookshop possibly—the Beacon of Light Bookshop on Polk. That's where I work.

DORIS. That's it. Sure—I think I once paid you for a *Reader's Digest*.

FELIX. Very possibly. I never look at the customers. Especially *Reader's Digest* customers.

DORIS. What's wrong with the *Reader's Digest?*

FELIX. Oh God—not now.

DORIS. What's the matter? The sun doesn't spit in anybody's face in the *Reader's Digest*, right?

FELIX. No. In the *Reader's Digest* mediocrity drools all over itself!

DORIS. I don't know what *that* means! . . . What do you think of Washington?

FELIX. What?

DORIS. "Doris Washington." (*She tries it with different in-*

flections.) Doris. Doris Washington . . . Miss Doris Washington. That's very common, isn't it?

FELIX. No question. I notice you favor the initial W.

DORIS. That's because my real name is Wilgus. It's a terrible name, but I would never think of giving up that W.

FELIX. Respect for family tradition. Good for you! What about "Wadsworth"?

DORIS. I used that. I was Doris Wadsworth for two weeks once, in Vegas, was it? Yeah, Vegas.

FELIX. I was Sigmund Freud in a girl's apartment one night for three hours.

DORIS. You know that's the second thing you said I didn't understand and I didn't get mad.

FELIX. What was the first?

DORIS. *Reader's Digest* drooling or something. I think I'm falling in love with you.

FELIX. With me—come on now—

DORIS. Believe it or not, you're my type. All the guys I fall in love with are weak in the body and strong in the head. And half the time they turn out to be—gay. That's my luck. You wanna kiss me?

[44]

FELIX. No.

DORIS. Try it.

FELIX. No thank you.

DORIS (*sighs*). Here I go again!

FELIX. You don't see any middle ground between no sex at all and wholesale copulation, do you?

DORIS. What does that mean, baby?

FELIX. You can make me very grateful to you by not calling me "baby."

DORIS. Okay, lover—how does "lover" strike you?

FELIX. I don't care for any of those amorous generic labels. I am an individual named Felix.

DORIS. I wouldn't say that name for a million dollars. You would make me very grateful by not saying it again. Also by not using those big words. You'll make me sore.

FELIX (*amused*). I'll watch it.

DORIS. I think you need a new name. It'll be good for you. You're an "M"—"Mark"—no—"Michael"—Michael, that's it!

[45]

FELIX. I'm staying with Felix—thank you.

DORIS. You're cute as hell— Did you ever go with a girl?

FELIX. As a matter of fact, I've been seeing one girl for almost two years.

DORIS. No kidding. Where is she?

FELIX. She's in New York right now.

DORIS. What does she look like?

FELIX. I'll show you. (*Picks up a slim book from the mantel.*)

DORIS. She's a writer?

FELIX. She's one of the finest poetesses in the country.

DORIS (*looking at the book*). Anne—(*mispronouncing it*) Weyderhaus?

FELIX. Weyderhaus.

DORIS (*turns book over—reads*). *September Leaves*—she looks very brainy.

FELIX. She is.

DORIS. She knows how to look it. That's for sure! I'm trying to picture her with a girl's hairdo.

[46]

FELIX. She likes to wear her hair that way. I assure you she's very much a woman.

DORIS. Well, okay. Who said she wasn't?

FELIX (*caught on the limb*). Well, I just wanted you to know.

DORIS (*shrugs*). That's between you and her. There's more than one way to skin a cat.

FELIX. Now what does that mean?

DORIS (*opening a book*). Just a saying. (*Looks at it.*) It don't rhyme, honey.

FELIX. No. In that respect it doesn't come up to Mother Goose.

DORIS. She'll flip when she hears about you having a girl in your place all night—

FELIX. No she won't. We don't have that kind of relationship.

DORIS. I bet. I can't wait to tell her, anyway—

FELIX. You're not serious.

DORIS. It's my duty. Guy cheating on his girl. Gotta hold society together.

FELIX. Now listen, you can't do that!

[47]

DORIS. What's the matter—you got no sense of humor?

FELIX. I thought you were serious.

DORIS. It's hard to tell when I'm kidding. I'm such a good actress.

FELIX. You really are.

DORIS. People are always saying to me, "Gee, Doris, we never know when you're kidding." And listen—about your story —I get sore at Shakespeare too—so it's probably a sign you're a genius—let's kiss and make up.

(*And before* FELIX *can move* DORIS *has thrown her arms around him.* FELIX *responds and the kiss develops some heat.* FELIX *leans over her getting lost in the kiss—then catches himself and breaks out of it. He's badly disturbed. He's lost the smug upper hand and is battling for his life from now on.*)

Hey! Whatever gave you the idea you were gay?

FELIX. I never had that idea. You had it.

DORIS. Wow! That's all I can say—wow! Where you running?

FELIX. I have to be at work at eight-thirty.

DORIS. We got plenty of time. Kiss me again.

[48]

FELIX. I've got to get some sleep—listen I have an idea—there's a radio in my bedroom—

DORIS (*happily*). Good!

FELIX. It's built into the headboard—so why don't you sleep in my bed?

DORIS (*happily*). Crazy.

FELIX. I'll sleep out here.

DORIS (*distastefully*). Swell! What's wrong, baby? I know you want to.

FELIX. I happen to be an intellectual. That means that I am not at the mercy of what I *want* to do.

DORIS. Groovy!

FELIX. Only animals are controlled by their appetites. Go on now. You can let the radio put you to sleep.

(DORIS *rises—showing him her legs.* FELIX *is on the ropes and* DORIS *knows it. She exits and he goes back to the sofa —sits down.* DORIS *appears at the door. She's teasing him now.*)

DORIS. Hey—it's a double bed.

FELIX. I know.

[49]

DORIS. I always feel so selfish sleeping alone in a double bed—
when there are people in China sleeping on the ground.

FELIX. Please go to sleep.

(*She shrugs and exits. He lies down—turns over restlessly
—looks to the bedroom. His eye falls on the book of poetry.
He puts the book away from him.*)

DORIS (*off stage*). How do you turn it on?

FELIX. Second knob from the right.

DORIS (*off stage*). Good night.

FELIX. Good night.

DORIS (*off stage*). Is that too loud?

FELIX. I can't even hear it.

DORIS (*off stage—singing it lovingly*). Good night.

FELIX. Good night! (*He turns over—turns over again—sits up
—picks up the book of poetry. He rises suddenly—goes to
the bookcase—shoves the book into it and comes back
to the sofa.*)

(DORIS *appears at the bedroom door.*)

DORIS. Michael, honey—

(FELIX *ignores her.*)

Honey—

(*He flops over restlessly on the sofa.*)

When you come in bring that blanket with you, will you, honey?

(DORIS *disappears into the bedroom.* FELIX *sits up. He realizes he's going into the bedroom—he panics suddenly in the realization of defeat.*)

FELIX (*shouting*). I am not an animal. I am a man of intellect. You can't do this to me.

DORIS. Hey, baby—not so loud!

FELIX. I am not "baby." I am not "honey." I am Felix, Felix, Felix, Felix, Felix! (*Exhausted by the outburst he flops on the sofa as* THE NEIGHBOR *knocks on the wall.* FELIX *addresses the wall, shouting.*) Felix! (*He stops—sighs. Looks at the blanket. Slowly he reaches for it and starts for the bedroom.*)

Blackout

ACT TWO

Scene 1

Morning light through the window. The phone is ringing —FELIX *staggers sleepily out of the bedroom—picks up the phone.*

FELIX. Hello—what? Oh, Victor—what time is it? . . . Oh— no—I'm not coming in today, Victor—yes . . . I don't know what it is . . . I think I'm fighting off a bug . . . no —I'll call one—yes—yes I will. Good-by, Victor. (*He hangs up—looks around the room.*)

DORIS (*off stage—sleepily*). Michael!

FELIX. Yes?

DORIS (*off stage*). What time is it?

FELIX. Nine forty-five.

DORIS (*off stage*). Who was that?

FELIX. Victor—the fellow who owns the bookshop.

(DORIS *appears at the door in her nightgown—she stretches in traditional feline contentment.* FELIX *prepares the coffeepot and takes oranges out of bag. She goes to* FELIX.)

[55]

DORIS. What did you tell him?

FELIX (*pulling away from her*). That I'm fighting off a bug.

DORIS. What are we doing today?

FELIX. I'm doing some research at the library.

DORIS. Let me do that—(*she takes the knife from* FELIX's *hand and cuts the oranges*). You sore at me?

FELIX. Of course I'm not sore at you.

DORIS. You hate yourself in the morning?

FELIX. No, I don't hate myself. Stop being foolish.

DORIS. I don't know about anybody else, but I'm in love. (*Singing.*) I'm in love with a wonderful guy.

(FELIX *has opened the door—taken in a bottle of milk and a newspaper. He folds newspaper open at the classified section.*)

Did you hear what I said? Hey, sexy—did you hear me?

FELIX (*running down the columns*). Unfurnished—unfurnished—furnished rooms—

DORIS (*hurt—trying to hide it*). I guess you don't want me to stay here—that's pretty obvious.

FELIX. Don't be ridiculous.

DORIS. Frankly, I don't like this place very much. I mean the way you got it fixed. It isn't very inviting.

FELIX. You weren't very invited.

DORIS. I liked you better last night. You're a very changeable fella, you know that?

FELIX. (*He finishes the coffee preparation and straightens the room during the dialogue.*) Do you always wake up overflowing with unsolicited character analysis?

DORIS (*an explosion of temper*). You watch your language, damn you! Far as I'm concerned you are talking to yourself and frankly I find you very enervating.

FELIX. Let me do that—you get dressed.

DORIS (*pushing him away*). I'm doing it. I'll be dressed and out of here in no time at all—I assure you.

(*As* FELIX *goes back to what he was doing, turning his back to her.*)

I can't stand people who don't look you in the eye when you're talking to them!

(*There's a moment of cold silence as* DORIS *squeezes the oranges and* FELIX *cleans ash trays. Then, her voice trembling:*) I should of slept in the park last night!

[57]

FELIX. Have you ever tried letting thirty seconds go by without talking?

DORIS. Have you ever tried dropping dead?

FELIX. What a rare combination of ladylike delicacy and penetrating wit. And to reply to it on its own high intellectual level—(*strums his lower lip with his forefinger and exits to bathroom*).

DORIS. Go on—play with yourself. Nobody cares—

FELIX. You know something—the quality of your conversation makes it hard to tell whether you're talking or vomiting.

DORIS. Now, that's clever. That should go in a story—right after the sun spits in the man's face. (DORIS *finishes one glass of juice—starts the second.*) I fall in love three or four times a week. It doesn't mean a thing. You hear me? You should see some of the stupid jerks I fall in love with!

(*There's the sound of the toilet flushing from the bathroom.*)

The same to you, mister! And you're so lousy in bed it's funny!

FELIX (*off stage*). I didn't hear you laughing.

DORIS. I was just showing common courtesy. I was acting.

FELIX (*off stage*). I've seen the role played much better.

DORIS. Drop dead!

FELIX (*off stage*). I've got the perfect name for you—Doris Watercloset.

DORIS. I've got the perfect name for you too—Felix Fruit! I can't wait to get out of here—you make me sick.

FELIX (*off stage*). The nauseation is mutual.

DORIS. That's your story! (*The juice is finished. She picks up the newspaper and looks at the ads—running her finger down the column. Suddenly she stops. The classified ads have thrown her back into the bleak pattern of her days.* FELIX *appears at the bathroom door. He's buttoning his shirt.*)

FELIX. Listen, would you go to see somebody about a job if I gave you a name and an address?

DORIS. I can get along very well without any help from you.

FELIX. That suits me.

DORIS (*mimicking him*). "That suits me." You sound like my goddam brother. What kind of a job?

FELIX. Working on hats.

DORIS. What kind of hats?

FELIX. Women's hats. A customer of mine, Mrs. Lucillian, makes hats to order—she has a shop on Columbus—she was in yesterday and mentioned that she needs a girl to help her.

DORIS. I don't know the first thing about hats.

FELIX. You don't have to, I don't think. She shows you what to do. Why don't you go and see her?

DORIS. It sounds like a drag. Working on hats.

FELIX. Forgive me—I forgot you have easier ways of earning money.

DORIS (*rising—livid*). I will not take that from you. I am a model. You get that through your big stupid brain and don't you ever forget it.

FELIX. All I said was—

DORIS. Whatever I might do on the side to stay alive is not what I am.

FELIX (*calmly smug*). I'm afraid it's what you do to pay your rent that classifies you. (FELIX *throws his smug line as he goes to the bedroom tucking in his shirt.*)

DORIS. All right—then what are you? What does that make you?

[60]

(FELIX *stops at the bedroom door momentarily.* DORIS *has struck a nerve. He exits to the bedroom.*)

(*Calling.*) Hey clerk! Clerk! *Reader's Digest,* please! Hey boy—which comic book do you recommend?

(*There is a silence from the bedroom.* DORIS *slumps unhappily on the sofa.* FELIX *enters from the bedroom, looking grim. He's putting on a coat sweater. During following dialogue he picks up a yellow legal pad and puts it into a leather envelope.*)

FELIX. You can take your time getting out. I won't be home until four.

DORIS. How could you be as sweet as you were last night and then wake up like such a monster? Would you mind very much telling a poor dumb girl just what happened—so she'll know . . . Did I say something? I say dopey things sometimes but I don't mean anything by it. (*She follows him as he crosses toward the door, stage right, in stony silence.*) You said something so beautiful to me—I bet you don't remember. It was the most beautiful thing anybody ever said to me. And I turned on the light so I could see your face.

(*He opens the door—exits. She holds it open—calling after him—angry.*) You looked happy! You looked happy— you fink!

Blackout

[61]

Scene 2

Four o'clock that afternoon. Door opens and FELIX *enters —takes off sweater, opens the closet door. Just as he does,* DORIS *pops out—she's determinedly gay.*

DORIS. Surprise!

FELIX. What are you doing here?

DORIS. I couldn't find a room.

FELIX. You mean you didn't look for one.

DORIS. Hey—you think that could have anything to do with it?

(FELIX *glares at her—goes into the bedroom and returns with the TV set—and starts for the door.* DORIS *pushes him. There's a short wrestling match.* FELIX *is no match for her. He falls helpless and winded on the sofa.*)

The first thing you're gonna do is join a gym.

(*As* FELIX *takes his briefcase and starts to pack it.*)

Where are you going?

[62]

FELIX. If you can't get the vermin out of your house, then you move out and leave the vermin in possession. You have no choice.

DORIS. What's the vermin? Is that me?

FELIX. Vermin—that means crawling insects.

DORIS. I know, but you can't insult me—it's impossible, you know why?

FELIX. Why are you doing this—why don't you get out? What's it going to get you?

DORIS. It's all your fault.

FELIX. All right—but—

DORIS. Oh I don't mean getting me thrown out of my room. I mean it's your fault I'm in love.

FELIX. You're insane.

DORIS. It's true—you made me love you. (*Sings.*) I didn't want to do it—

FELIX. What do I have to do to get rid of you? I'll give you ten dollars.

DORIS. Make it fifty million—that's how much it'll cost you to get rid of me—not a penny less. Hey—I thought you were going to move out and leave the vermin in possession—what happened?

FELIX. No. I will not let you put me out of my home.

DORIS. Good for you! I would have lost all respect for you if you left.

FELIX. How long are you planning to stay?

DORIS. How should I know? I'm stuck here. (*Sings.*) I'm just a prisoner of love. Notice I'm singing all the time—I always do that when I'm in love.

FELIX. You're an imbecile.

DORIS. Okay. Fine! See—you can't insult a person who's in love. You can't do anything to them, because they're so light—you can throw them off the roof and they'll float to the ground.

FELIX. Will you stop talking about love—I've never heard such mindless drivel in my life.

DORIS. Listen, I know a lot about love.

FELIX. That thing you fall in and out of three or four times a week is not love. Neither is that thing you sell.

DORIS. Now don't be nasty, honey. This is different. I love you in a very deep quiet way—like a river.

[64]

FELIX. Like a river! (*Shouting.*) You mean like a sewer!

DORIS. Now don't get worked up, darling. You tell me what love is. Go ahead, sweetheart—I'm listening. Is it when you get mad and yell at somebody like you're yelling at me?

FELIX (*shouting*). No, it is not!

DORIS. You better calm down . . .

FELIX (*fighting for self-control*). You upset me. I admit it. You're an animal. You're so foreign to anything that's important to me. Don't you understand?—you personify what I hate.

DORIS. You didn't hate it last night.

FELIX. That's what disgusts me. All my life I fought that animal taint. It's like finding a fungus you loathe growing on your own skin!

DORIS (*shaken badly*). Oh, that's a disgusting thing to call somebody—"fungus"!

FELIX. I didn't call you that.

DORIS. Sure—I'm some slimy, moldy fungus, right?

FELIX. I didn't say that.

[65]

DORIS. Oh yes you did say that!

FELIX. All right, I said it! I mean it! Now will you get out—will you go?

DORIS. I never met anybody in my life that made me feel so cheap and dirty.

FELIX. Then get out of here.

DORIS. I don't understand why I love you.

FELIX. Get out! I hate you!

DORIS. Not as much as I hate you!

FELIX. Then get out! Get out!

DORIS. No! I'm gonna stay here and hate you right to your face!

FELIX. All right, then I'm going.

DORIS. Fine. Great. Go on.

FELIX. It's the only way.

DORIS. Well go on—get out.

FELIX. What do you mean, "get out"? This is my home. I live here. Don't you tell me to get out.

DORIS. Well, I'm not getting out. You can try to throw me out
if you want to.

FELIX. I wouldn't dirty my hands.

DORIS. I wouldn't want your slimy hands on me.

FELIX. I ought to turn you over to the police.

DORIS. Fine. Why don't you?

FELIX. That's what I should do.

DORIS. Go ahead. Call them.

FELIX. That's what I'll do. That's just what I'll do!

DORIS. Go ahead.

FELIX. That's just exactly what I'm going to do!

DORIS. All right. Fine. You do that.

FELIX. You bet I will. You can just bet on it!

DORIS. You call the police. You do that. It's fine with me.

FELIX. Don't you for a moment think I won't!

DORIS. Oh you'd do it!

FELIX. You bet I would. And that's just what I'm going to do.

DORIS. Fine. You turn me in. You do that. You're the man to do it.

FELIX. I most certainly am and that's what I'm going to do!

Blackout

Scene 3

FELIX (*on telephone*). Nothing serious, Victor. No—I'm a little tired. I had a very bad time last night. No—I hate to take them, they're enervating. Thank you, but I'll be fine by twelve or so. I'll come in then.

(*Lights come up slowly. Morning light through the window.* DORIS *stands near* FELIX, *peering at him through the binoculars.*)

DORIS. Ooh, look at the big man.

(*He ignores her.*)

Don't you love me? Oh, that's right—only in the bedroom. I forgot—it depends on what room we're in. Let's take a shower together. I want to find out how you feel about me in the bathroom.

FELIX. Doris—I'm not coming back to this apartment tonight. I mean it.

DORIS. Honey—what are you fighting? Why don't you take it easy? (*She tries to embrace him— He pushes her off, knocking the orange out of her hand.* DORIS *laughs, picks up the orange.*) You better bring some more oranges. We're running out.

FELIX. I won't be coming back. Did you hear me?

DORIS (*humoring a child*). Sure. You'll be back after work to pack your things though?

(*Silence from* FELIX.)

Would you like me to pack for you and have it ready?

FELIX. Shut up.

DORIS. I could put it all outside the door so you wouldn't even have to come inside.

FELIX. Your humor is like you are—crude and clumsy.

DORIS (*going to him—tenderly*). Baby—why don't you stop—

FELIX. If you call me "baby" once more, I'll—(*looks around desperately*) I'll smash your television set.

DORIS (*goes to him—feels his head*). I think you've got a fever.

FELIX (*looking to Heaven*). Oh God! Are you listening—are you laughing? She says I've got a fever.

DORIS. You're not going to work today—you're getting right back into bed.

[70]

FELIX (*to Heaven*). Do you hear? The tower of my mind is crashing down—wrecked by a termite—and now the termite is putting me to bed! God—do something!

(*She's pushing and pulling him to the sofa.*)

DORIS. Don't talk to God that way. He'll strike you dead.

FELIX. Oh no! Not while He's having so much fun with me!

(*She pushes him down on the sofa—feels his head again.*)

DORIS. Does it hurt any place?

FELIX. Listen—I'm going to beg you—please—go away—please leave me alone.

DORIS (*feeling his throat*). Does this hurt?

FELIX. You're grinding your heel in my raw soul. That is what hurts.

DORIS. Wow! That's good! You ought to use that in a story.

FELIX (*weakly*). You must go away. Why won't you go away? Tell me why—!

DORIS. Because, sweetheart—I can make you happy—I do make you happy—if you'll only let me—

FELIX. No—no—you make me miserable.

[71]

DORIS. But baby . . .

FELIX. "Baby" you make happy, yes—but "Felix" you make miserable and that's me—Felix—I am Felix. Will you listen to me? I am not "baby." I don't want to be "baby."

DORIS. I wish you'd go to bed. Do you have a thermometer?

FELIX. It's a nightmare—I'm caught in a fog—I'm screaming! But I can't make a sound!

DORIS. Lie down on the sofa.

(*Limp,* FELIX *flops down on the sofa.*)

FELIX. What's the use?

DORIS. That's my boy.

FELIX. Yes. That's your boy. I confess. Felix unmasked. Felix captured and brought to justice—"baby—honey—sweetheart" alias "Felix".

DORIS. Now just relax. (*She feels his forehead again.*) Does it hurt any place?

FELIX. No. All the nerves have died.

DORIS. Now be serious. Is your throat sore? Do you have a headache? Should I call the doctor?

FELIX. That's ridiculous! The disease never calls the doctor.

DORIS. Now don't say nasty things! Be nice.

FELIX (*rising hysteria*). Nice? You're absolutely right! Now that I have come to live in Niceville I must do as the nice people do—I must be nice. "Baby sweetheart" must be nice.

DORIS (*beginning to be afraid*). You're absolutely crazy. I never heard such crazy talk in my life.

FELIX. You're right again. Baby must not speak the language of Felix. Felix the mind is dead. Long live baby!

DORIS. Please stop it.

FELIX. Call me "baby"—say, "Please stop it, baby"—go on.

DORIS. I don't want to.

FELIX. Why not—that's who I am—I'm baby.

DORIS. Please, honey, you're scaring me.

FELIX. Yes—yes—sorry—that's because I'm not talking baby's language. How's this (*tough:*) What do you say we feed the face, sweetie, and then we can hop into the sack and knock off a quickie. Let's ball. Let's get down in the slime and roll around in it. Let's have a little poon-tang. Let's hump.

[73]

(As DORIS *withdraws from him.*)

That's it, hump, hump, hump.

DORIS (*completely depressed by now*). All right—all right, you win.

FELIX. I win? What do I win?

DORIS. I'm going. (*She exits to bedroom; then from off stage:*) I'll come back later to get my things. When you're not here.

FELIX (*calls*). Are you really going, baby?

DORIS. That's what you want, isn't it?

FELIX. It's not my first choice. My first choice is for you never to have come. Could I have that?

DORIS. You sure fooled me. I thought I had you figured.

FELIX. You did—I'm the one I had fooled.

DORIS (*opens the door*). I'll call you tonight when I get set and let you know where I am.

FELIX. Don't call.

DORIS. Don't be such a baby. You can always hang up on me if you don't want to talk to me.

[74]

FELIX. I won't be here.

DORIS. You better take care of yourself or you're gonna be sick. You hear me?

FELIX (*wryly*). I'll take an aspirin.

DORIS. Good idea—no. There's some fizz powder on the dresser. It gets into the bloodstream seconds faster than aspirin.

FELIX. I grew up with aspirin. I refuse to believe there's a short-cut aspirin doesn't know about.

DORIS. Just the same—take that powder. And I'll call you tonight.

FELIX (*shouting, as* DORIS *exits*). I won't be here!

(*Alone now,* FELIX *sits for a moment staring at the floor. He puts his hands to his face in a stab of panic. He rises and paces rapidly. He goes to the window. His eyes fall on the binoculars. He picks them up—turns them over— carries them to the stage left platform and lays them on the corner. He goes to the sink and opens the drawer, takes out a hammer, and goes to them. He kneels and systematically pounds the binoculars to pieces as:*)

Curtain falls

Scene 4

Two o'clock the following morning.

The room is dark. We hear FELIX's *footsteps and his key in the lock. The door opens and he enters. Turns on the light. His eyes go first to the bedroom door. Then to the floor where* DORIS's *television set still occupies its spot.*

FELIX (*addressing the bedroom door as he crosses to it*). I see you couldn't find a room again. I should have known you were lying. What made me think you'd keep your word? You don't know how to—(*He has exited to bedroom on the last words. There's a pause.*)

(*Continued off stage.*) Doris! Doris——?

(FELIX *comes slowly out of the bedroom. He goes to the closet door—opens it—looks inside—then the bathroom door—opens it and looks inside—closes the door.* DORIS *has gone. He goes to the sofa—sits—looking at the TV set. The phone rings. He reaches for it—pulls back—he rises and lights a cigarette nervously as the phone continues to ring. It's a slow patient ring with all the time in the world. Finally* FELIX *picks it up with an impulsive swoop.*)

[76]

(*Angry.*) Hello. (*On phone—continued.*) Oh—nothing, Victor—I just got home. I went to a movie . . . Angry— why should I get angry at a telephone? Helpless tool of a monopoly! What? . . . Oh—when did she call? What was the number? 4–6792. (*He writes it down. Then, to Victor.*) Good night. (*Hangs up.*)

(*He paces, miserable. He stops at the phone, picks it up, picks up the phone number, puts it down. Picks it up again and dials . . . waits. He hears* DORIS *say "Hello" and he panics.*)

Wrong number.

(*He slams the receiver down and paces—raging at himself. Stops at the phone. Picks it up again, dials, waits—and panics once more.*)

Wrong number!

(*Slams down the receiver. He's so angry with himself he slaps his face hard enough to stagger himself. Then gathers all his courage. Deliberately and resolutely picks up the phone and dials.*)

Hello, Doris? . . . Felix. I hope I didn't wake you . . . No! Wrong numbers, huh? . . . That's a shame. I guess at this hour of the morning there's an awful lot of drunk dialing. Drunk dialing! You know, like drunk driving—it's a joke. I know there's nothing funny about drunk driving. That isn't what I meant— Oh, forget it. Well I just got home. You left your television set . . . Oh . . . Tell him to come after three . . . How do you like your room? That's a shame! Well don't let it depress you—you'll be on your feet again in no time . . . No, it was not a crack! You mustn't be so damn sensitive . . . All right, all right. Listen, I've been doing a lot of thinking and I wanted to talk to you . . . Not on the phone . . . Well, I've been thinking and I realized that we got off on the wrong foot, you and I and it was silly and I think we can be friends and I think our relationship must be re-established on a different basis . . . No. They just sound big over the phone. Look, I thought if you weren't doing anything right now . . .

(*He gets a disappointing response to this.*)

Oh . . . yes—well how about having lunch with me . . . Oh . . . well what are you doing for . . . I see. Yes . . . Yes . . . That won't give us much time . . . Yes. All right, I'll look for you around six . . . I hope you don't . . . Doris? . . . Hello . . . Doris?

(DORIS *has hung up.* FELIX *replaces the receiver. He sighs deeply. Looks around the room. He crosses right—turns on the table lamp. Crosses down to straighten out the coffee table, sits on the couch. Takes radio off the coffee table and places it on the floor. As the radio touches the floor it bursts into sound—a rock and roll recording from an all-night disc jockey. And as the music drones on,* FELIX *lies on the sofa on his side, wide-eyed and sleepless.*)

Blackout

[78]

Scene 5

Six P.M. *that day. The room is empty. The front door is ajar. There's a knock and* DORIS *sticks her head through.*

DORIS. Anybody home?

FELIX (*in bathroom*). Is it still raining?

DORIS (*still at door*). No, it stopped.

FELIX (*off stage*). Paper said it would rain all night.

DORIS. Yeah.

FELIX (*off stage*). I guess the rain doesn't read the paper. There's some scotch on the table.

DORIS. Where'd you get this?

FELIX (*off stage*). Bought it.

DORIS. How come?

FELIX (*off stage*). Not enough nerve to steal it, I suppose. Take your coat off. (*He enters from bedroom, his hair slicked for the occasion.*) I like your dress.

[79]

DORIS. The color's good, but it flattens me out a little in the bust. You don't look so good.

FELIX. I had a hard day. Listen— I wanted to talk to you, Doris. It's a little embarrassing— I wanted to apologize for my emotional behavior yesterday morning.

DORIS. Forget it. It was my fault— I guess I needled you.

FELIX. No. The lance is not the cause of the infection it exposes. The fact that—

DORIS (*stopping him*). Wait a minute—(*thinks for a second— then triumphantly:*) You know, I understand that!

FELIX. Of course—naturally. Doris, you're a bright girl. Remember I told you that soon after we met?

DORIS. Yes, you did. You said I wasn't dumb.

FELIX. And that's exactly what I want to talk to you about. After you left I used some good solid logic. It saved my life.

DORIS. That sounds good.

FELIX. Well, the fact is, I have lived almost thirty years as a logical man. My religion was the reason. The mind. It's the only thing I believe in. And it has given me a lonely life.

DORIS. I thought you were older than thirty.

FELIX. I'll be thirty in October. Fact number two—I felt a very powerful attraction to a girl—you—very powerful all right —put the facts through the logic—there's only one answer —I had to be attracted by one thing in you.

DORIS. Well, listen—

FELIX. Your mind!

DORIS. You're kidding.

FELIX. Doesn't it sound logical?

DORIS. It may be logical, but it doesn't make sense.

FELIX. I realized suddenly that I'm not attracted to you at all as an animal. Don't you see—I couldn't be. It's your trapped intelligence calling out for help that drew me so strongly.

DORIS. You're all excited and happy. Gee, I'm glad. You were in such bad shape yesterday you had me scared.

FELIX. That was insane grief. Premature grief for Felix the mind. I was very rough on you. I feel like dying when I think of the things I said to you. Can you forgive me? Can we be friends—non-physical friends, of course.

DORIS. Non-physical?

[81]

FELIX. I'm going to save you, Doris.

DORIS. May I ask from what?

FELIX. From circumstances that have kept you from using your mind. You're in a jungle. I'm going to cut through all that rotting growth and rescue you.

DORIS. I feel like Sleeping Beauty with that forest around her.

FELIX. Yes—yes—that's wonderful! The sleeping beauty of the mind.

DORIS. Wonderful?

FELIX. Without training—your unhindered natural imagination reaches for metaphor—oh Doris—do you know how exciting that is to a man of intellect?

DORIS. What's "metaphor"?

FELIX. Metaphor is—no—there—(*points to the dictionary*) look it up for yourself. Go—discover a word! M-e-t-a-p-h-o-r.

DORIS. Not me—I hate dictionaries.

FELIX. Why? You like words.

DORIS. Yeah, but in the dictionary they're so, I don't know—dead.

[82]

FELIX. Dead—oh my God, of course! Laid out—dissected—by the cataloguing mind! A mortuary of words—Doris, that's wonderful!

DORIS. You mean I did it again? I can't tell you how surprised I am.

FELIX. I felt it in you—I sensed it, didn't I?

DORIS. Yes, you did—you said something about it.

FELIX. I know—I know.

DORIS (*catching the artificial excitement*). It was very smart of you to notice—most people don't notice—*I* never noticed! Gosh, think of all the smart things I must of said without realizing!

FELIX. Yes—a flower born to blush unseen—wasting your sweetness on the desert air.

DORIS. That's like poetry.

FELIX. It is poetry. Famous poetry.

DORIS. Hey—I spotted it, didn't I?

(As DORIS *starts to sparkle with excitement*, FELIX *is aroused*.)

[83]

FELIX. Of course you spotted it. Like a thirsty root spots water—

DORIS. Did I ever tell you about the essay I wrote in school?

FELIX. I'd love to read it.

DORIS. I lost it.

FELIX. That's all right—you'll write others.

DORIS. You think so?

FELIX. Why not? Why not?

DORIS. I used to think I had a brain. But people keep calling you stupid, you know—year after year.

FELIX. Stupid people.

DORIS. My goddam brother. From morning to night—"stupid-stupid-stupid." Well, after a while you figure where there's smoke there's fire—you know?

FELIX. Of course. A sensitive nature like yours is no match for a bully.

DORIS. Sensitive! Boy you put your finger on it! How did you know I was sensitive?

FELIX. You had to be—that's the price of a thinking mind— sensitivity.

DORIS. It is?

FELIX. Yes.

DORIS. Well, I'm sure sensitive, all right. I cry at the drop of a hat. Well, you saw the way I carried on here yesterday—

FELIX. Yes.

DORIS. Over nothing at all. Did you ever see sensitive like that?

FELIX. I should have known. I should have realized why I was drawn to you.

DORIS. I was always ashamed of myself for crying so much. That means you're smart, huh?

FELIX. It means—that's right—it means you're smart.

DORIS. I always thought I was such a dope—crying over nothing.

FELIX. Dopes don't cry. They have no pride. Dopes are not vulnerable.

DORIS. Pride—I got a lot of that.

FELIX. Of course you have.

[85]

DORIS. My brother always said to me that I had too much pride.

FELIX. Is that the "goddam" brother?

DORIS. No—the older one.

FELIX. Well, you can't have too much pride. Pride constructs dignity and lives in it.

DORIS. "Pride constructs dignity and lives in it"? Poetry—right?

FELIX. It's from an essay of mine.

DORIS. Oh. Well, it sounds like poetry.

FELIX. Thank you.

DORIS. I'll bet you're a wonderful writer.

FELIX. You didn't care for my short story. Remember?

DORIS. When? Oh—the sun spitting in the guy's face—well, I was mad at you—I was just getting back at you.

FELIX. Well, it doesn't matter.

DORIS. It grows on you. I can see it, you know—

FELIX. What's that?

DORIS (*acting out the rising sun*). The sun—like a big face. It looks up real slow over the edge of the world and it goes—pttt. (*She makes a soft spitting sound with her lips.*)

FELIX. That's very imaginative of you.

DORIS. Well, it's just good writing, that's all—it makes you see it.

FELIX. Thank you.

DORIS. Gee, I'm so excited! I'm shivering—look at me.

FELIX. Would you like a drink?

DORIS. I got one.

FELIX (*putting his arm around her*). Are you cold?

DORIS. No—I don't know what it is—excitement I guess.

FELIX. I know what it is. It's the first shock of childbirth.

DORIS. Bite your tongue!

FELIX (*fondles and nuzzles her*). No—I mean *you're* being born. *You*—

DORIS. Yeah—I see what you mean—I'm being born—you know what I'm doing? I'm entering into a new world.

[87]

(*He kisses her on the cheek.*)

You didn't hear what I said—

FELIX. What?

DORIS. I'm entering into a new world.

FELIX. I heard you. It's true, welcome to the world of the intellect. (*He kisses her on the neck.*)

DORIS. I'm beginning to talk like you a little—did you notice—hey—what are you doing—I wanna talk.

FELIX (*continuing to make love to her*). I want to hear you talk, don't stop.

DORIS. Felix—cut that out—

FELIX. Talk—I'm listening.

DORIS. We're intellectuals—we're non-physicals, remember?

FELIX. This isn't physical. That's what makes it so exciting—don't you see?

DORIS. I don't think so.

FELIX. That's what draws us together—not the attraction of bodies, but the excitement of two live—healthy—exuberant minds—calling hungrily to one another!

[88]

DORIS. Oh.

FELIX. It's an irresistible intellectual attraction. (*He throws himself at her, hungrily.*)

DORIS. Is that what this is—intellectual?

FELIX. Of course.

DORIS. It's our minds?

FELIX (*in a frenzy of self-delusion*). Yes—yes.

DORIS (*starting to respond*). It's not the usual thing?

FELIX. No—no—of course not—

DORIS. You know something—it's every bit as good!

Blackout

Scene 6

Three weeks later. Nobody home. The TV set is back. We hear running footsteps up the stairs. The door is opened with a key and DORIS *bursts into the room. She's carrying an expensive portable radio. She shoves the radio under the coffee table—pulls off her sweater—throws it onto a chair—snatches up a book—we hear* FELIX's *footsteps on the stairs outside as* DORIS *falls onto the sofa and becomes absorbed in the book.* FELIX *opens the door with his key and enters.*

DORIS. Hi, sweetie.

FELIX (*very quiet. He's holding down the lid on boiling indignation*). Hello.

DORIS. Hey, what's this? We've only been living in sin for three weeks and already you don't kiss me "hello" any more?

FELIX. I had a hard day. Have you been out?

DORIS. Only for lunch. Hey, you wanna check the breakfast dishes? I'll give you a half a buck you find any dirt or any dried soap this time!

FELIX. Later. I saw somebody enter the building as I got off the bus. I thought it was you.

[90]

DORIS. Must have been the girl downstairs. You hungry, sweetie?

FELIX. No, I've got a headache. (*Looking at her book.*) Still on chapter two?

DORIS. I had an awful lot of words to look up.

FELIX (*going to the dictionary, looks at it*). It wasn't the girl downstairs.

DORIS. Who? Oh—you want something for your headache?

FELIX. No, thank you. I'm enjoying it.

DORIS. Honest—some of the things you say sometimes.

FELIX. Have you been working with your word for the day?

DORIS. Oh—"impeccable"—sure—(*sneaking a look at her pad*) "Impeccable—without a fault—incapable of doing wrong." Now, used in a sentence—let's see. (*Looking around.*) Oh —when the typewriter got back from the repair shop, it was impeccable.

FELIX. No—that's wrong.

DORIS. Why?

FELIX. In three weeks I don't think you've assimilated two new words.

DORIS. Oh, come on—sure I have. Hey what's the matter with you tonight?

FELIX. Have you been to the dictionary today?

DORIS. Sure—I told you.

FELIX. Yes. (*He's been taking off his tie—he sees the radio under the coffee table. He stands up.*) Where'd you get the radio?

DORIS. Oh—I picked it up at the junk shop—three bucks.

FELIX (*going to bedroom*). Good.

DORIS. I don't even know if it works.

FELIX (*exits to bedroom*). It looks brand new to me.

DORIS (*drags the set out—dumps the ash tray on it, rubs in the ashes—spits—scratches it with the ash tray as she talks*). It's practically an antique—made in the year one. I think I got taken but I needed a radio for out here. You have to play that one in the bed so loud if you wanna hear it out here and my other one keeps conking out—so I figured— what the hell—I'd take a chance—sometimes these old beat-up sets play as good as a new one.

(*She abruptly drops the aging process as* FELIX *comes out of the bedroom. He has taken off his coat.*)

[92]

FELIX. How many times did you say you used the dictionary today?

DORIS. I don't know. What's wrong, honey?

FELIX. Please go over to the dictionary and look at it closely.

DORIS (*goes and looks at the dictionary*). What am I supposed to see?

FELIX. Look at the edges—at the top—

DORIS. What's this? (*Peeling off a strip of Scotch tape.*)

FELIX. That is a strip of Scotch tape. It's been there for two days. Undisturbed. Where were you this afternoon?

DORIS. That's such a nasty thing to do.

FELIX. Where were you yesterday afternoon?

DORIS. I do not care for the tone of your voice.

FELIX. Where did you get the dirty but brand new radio?

DORIS. I'm warning you—stop it—this warning will not be repeated.

FELIX. We're not going to fight. We're going to have an honest unemotional discussion.

[93]

DORIS. Yeah? So you start out by calling me a liar.

FELIX. I did not call you a liar. I'm not going to lose my temper.

DORIS. You might as well. I'm gonna lose mine!

FELIX. Would you care to tell me what's wrong?

DORIS. What's wrong? You're a creep that puts Scotch tape on the dictionary—you know that word—"creep"? Used in a sentence: "Fred Sherman is a big creep."

FELIX (*starting at "Fred"*). What did you call me?

DORIS. It's your name. Fred—Freddie—I thought that would jar your apricots! I found your yearbook from school— Fred Sherman. You didn't tell me you changed your name, did you. You creep. I'm sorry—pardon my language, but you are a creep.

FELIX. It's all right—it's a step up from "fink". Congratulations —now—I'd like to hear why you feel you have to sneak out afternoons and lie to me.

DORIS. I just got bored. I had to get out. Look—I tried. I tried working on hats. I tried looking for a job, right? I tried.

FELIX. Have you been plying your old trade?

DORIS. Have I been what? No, I haven't. I told you I was through doing that.

FELIX. Where'd you get the radio?

DORIS. I collected some money. Somebody owed me some money and they paid me.

FELIX. I see. Why didn't you tell me that?

DORIS. Because I knew you wouldn't believe it. I knew what you'd think.

FELIX. I see.

DORIS. Don't say, "I see," like you were looking through your lousy spyglasses. Listen—why don't you stop trying to make out like you're a human being? I mean the strain must be terrible—why don't you just relax and admit you're God and you know all about everything?

FELIX. Why did you have to lie? I just want to know why you lied to me about going out and about looking up words.

DORIS. Because I'm a liar, okay?

FELIX. Why didn't you tell me?

DORIS. Why didn't you tell me you changed your name from "Fred" to "Felix"?

FELIX (*ignoring her question*). I'm very sad. You had a chance to do something important for yourself and you're quitting. You're not giving yourself a chance.

DORIS. I gave myself a chance—you had me going there for a while, but it's silly. I'm a dope and that's all there is to it.

FELIX. You're not a dope. You're a bright girl.

DORIS. Not when it comes to dictionaries and the history of philosophy, I'm not. (*Indicates the book she was reading.*)

FELIX. You have a potential capacity for—

DORIS (*interrupting*). No, I don't have any potential anything.

FELIX (*losing the fight against his temper*). Don't interrupt me—who do you think is better qualified to judge mental capacity—you or I?

DORIS. You—

FELIX. Then why are you arguing with me?

DORIS. Felix, I—

FELIX. Would I be wasting my time with you if you didn't have a brain?

DORIS. Felix—

FELIX. Do you think an intellectual such as myself would waste his time with a dumbbell?

DORIS. Felix, I know myself—you can't tell me—

FELIX. I tell you you're a very intelligent girl, and you'd know it yourself if you weren't so damned stupid!

DORIS. I am not stupid! I've got good healthy everyday brains. I haven't got your kind of brains and I'm glad, because I'm gonna tell you something—I think your brains are rotten!

FELIX. Ah—the cat turns inevitably and bares her atavistic fangs.

DORIS. To use those ugly, lonely words nobody else uses—that's all your brains are good for. To keep people away because you're scared to death of people!

FELIX. She spits in inarticulate fury.

DORIS. You know what your brains are good for? To make up your own lousy little language that the rest of the world can't even understand.

FELIX. Well, all right—stay with the rest of the world—don't let anybody make you a foreigner there by teaching you to speak the English language!

DORIS (*going to closet*). What a dope I was to listen to you.

[97]

(*Mimicking him.*) "I'm gonna save you, Doris!" (*In her own voice.*) You are such a phony, I can't believe it. You don't write for money, but you keep sending your junk to magazines, don't you? And you keep getting it sent back, don't you? Meanwhile all you got is a phony job, a phony girl friend, a phony apartment, and a phony bunch of words! (*She has taken the suitcase from the closet and started to throw garments into it as she talks.*)

FELIX. What are you doing?

DORIS. What does it look like I'm doing?

FELIX (*quietly*). Now don't get washed away. Think, Doris. Try to understand one basic thing. Try to hold on to what I see in you.

DORIS (*yelling*). You see nothing! You don't see me at all! You don't see anything. Because even your eyes are phony!

(*Knock on the wall.* DORIS *addresses the wall; yelling*)

I'll be through in a minute!

(*To* FELIX.) You know what you see in me. You never had a girl that made you feel like a big man in bed—that's all.

FELIX. Doris—

[98]

DORIS (*interrupting*). Well, I want to tell you something about what a hot stud you think you are in the sack—

FELIX. Don't say it, Doris—

DORIS. You leave me cold, Fred. You're nothing at all.

FELIX. You're raising your voice.

DORIS. You do nothing to me, Freddie, you only think you do. You know why?

FELIX. I know—you're a great actress and to you that bed is theatre in the round—I know all about it—well now I'm going to tell you something—I don't *leave* you cold—I *find* you cold—"frigid"— Is that word in your meager stock?

DORIS. Drop dead.

FELIX. Sure you're an actress in bed—because you can't be a woman.

DORIS. With a man I can, Fred—Freddie it takes a man.

FELIX. Sometimes. Even with fantasies, and dirty words and the guilty stink of the sewer you can only sometimes whip yourself into a parody of passion—sometimes! Isn't that right?

DORIS. Stop yelling. Nobody's listening to you. (*She's closing the suitcase.*)

FELIX. All right. You're lost. Good-by. I tried.

DORIS. Now try shutting up. I'll send for the TV. I'll send a man! Take a good look at him.

FELIX (*follows her to the door*). No matter where you go or what you do or what you call yourself—you are now and forever a whore named Doris Wilgus.

DORIS. Okay. And what are you now and forever? A miserable magazine peddler named Freddie Sherman and a lousy writer and you always will be and you wanna know why— (*hitting him deliberately with every word*) because, God damn it! the—sun—does—not—spit!

Blackout

ACT THREE

Scene 1

One week later. Afternoon. FELIX *is asleep on the couch—face down—all his clothing on—the bottle of scotch is on the floor, all gone but for an inch or so.* FELIX *stirs and awakens painfully. He takes four or five oranges from a drawer and cuts one in half—cuts his finger—drops the knife—looks at the cut —puts the finger in his mouth and crosses to the bathroom. Just after he exits to the bathroom, there's a knock at the door.*

FELIX (*off stage*). Come in.

(*There's a key in the lock and the door opens and* DORIS *enters. She comes into the room as* FELIX *enters from the bathroom—his finger in his mouth—holding an adhesive bandage in his other hand. They look at each other for a frozen instant.*)

I cut myself.

DORIS (*reaching for the adhesive bandage*). Let me open that.

FELIX (*handing it to her*). Thank you.

DORIS. How'd you do it?

[103]

FELIX. Cutting oranges.

(*In this exchange*, DORIS's *eyes are lowered to the cut finger*. FELIX *looks at her face*.)

DORIS. Orange juice at five o'clock in the afternoon?

FELIX. I was thinking of having Shredded Wheat for dinner.

DORIS (*putting the adhesive bandage on the cut*). Did you put anything on it?

FELIX. No. It's a medicated adhesive bandage.

DORIS. Do you have a lot of confidence in medicated adhesive bandages? I don't. This friend of mine got an infection from an adhesive bandage once.

FELIX. I'm very fatalistic about those things.

DORIS. Oh.

FELIX. I figure an adhesive bandage's either got your name on it or it hasn't.

DORIS. You're probably right. I'm a terrible worrier.

FELIX. No, you're right. It's better to be safe than sorry.

DORIS. Yes, but it's no good to live in fear. You can get killed crossing the street.

FELIX. Fools rush in where angels fear to tread.

DORIS. I beg your pardon— I don't follow that.

FELIX. I didn't follow it either.

DORIS. Let me make your orange juice for you.

FELIX. No—don't—don't bother—

DORIS (*starts to make juice*). I got time— I found this key to the apartment. I was in the neighborhood and I thought you might be needing an extra key.

FELIX. I've been getting by with the one. How's Allen?

DORIS. Allen?

FELIX. That nice looking fellow who picked up your television set.

DORIS. Oh, Aaron—you said "Allen." He's all right. He's married to my friend Barbara.

FELIX. Oh, nice chap.

DORIS. Yes—how's Anne? Back from New York yet?

FELIX. Yes. She's fine—I guess. I haven't seen her.

[105]

DORIS. By the way, do you like this suit? (*She turns away from the squeezer to show it.*)

FELIX. Very much. Is it new?

DORIS. Yes—I found this little shop on Filbert. It's real small but they have impeccable taste. (*A side glance to see the effect of "impeccable" on* FELIX.)

FELIX. That's very good.

DORIS. You notice I've assimilated "impeccable."

FELIX. Very good.

DORIS. I had to get some clothes for my new job. I'm a receptionist.

FELIX. Oh—good.

DORIS. It's a place called Ganshaver Brothers. Custom wallpaper. It's supposed to be for decorators only, but anybody can get in really.

FELIX. It sounds fine.

DORIS. And of course it gives me plenty of time for my reading. By the way, have you read *Oliver Twist* by Charles Dickens?

FELIX. Yes.

DORIS. He writes somewhat on the style of Somerset Maugham, don't you think?

FELIX. I think he steals from him.

DORIS. Yes, I think so, too. And, oh yes, I met this photographer who's taking pictures of me—you know for the model agencies. He's only charging me for his materials and labor and he really digs me—he's doing a layout—six different expressions—he wants to put it in a folder and call it "Doris Wheeler—Girl of a Thousand Moods." (*Pouring the juice from the squeezer.*) What do you think of "Wheeler"?

FELIX. I like it.

(*There's more juice than the glass will hold—*DORIS *takes another glass and pours the small surplus into it. She hands the full glass to* FELIX. *All this under dialogue.*)

DORIS. And what's new with you? How's your writing?

FELIX. It's legible.

DORIS. Oh good—I guess— (*Sipping her juice.*) Boy, you're right about fresh orange juice. It has an impeccable taste.

(DORIS *looks at* FELIX *over the edge of the glass—she covers her nervousness by sipping the juice.* FELIX *looks at her steadily for a moment. She smiles a nervous hopeful confused little smile.*)

[107]

FELIX. Why did you come back?

DORIS. I've assimilated three new words—"intricate," "belligerent," and "embellish." You wanna hear me use them in a sentence?

FELIX. No.

DORIS. It's not hard. You were right. I wasn't giving myself a chance. (*She has gone to the table—picks up a manuscript with a letter attached.*) Oh, you finally got your story back from that big shot. With a letter and everything. (*She reads the letter.*)

FELIX. Doris—why did you come back?

DORIS. What does he mean "counterfeit emotions and artificial images"?

FELIX. He means the sun doesn't spit.

DORIS (*reading*). He's sorry! (*Throws down the manuscript.*) Who the hell does he think he is!?

FELIX. Doris, why did you come back?

DORIS (*looking away from him*). I never had anybody like you in love with me before. I'll never find anybody like you again.

FELIX. You mean somebody who'll try to change you and then say rotten things to you because he can't change you?

DORIS. Oh, I don't care about that—I think you're a talented sweet wonderful man.

FELIX. You are disgusting, do you know that?

DORIS. Don't be mean to me—please.

FELIX. Why not? That's what you came for. Don't you know you came back for that?

DORIS. No, I didn't—

FELIX. Of course you did—why else but to be insulted? "Sweet wonderful man" she calls me! Have you forgotten the things we said to each other? Didn't any of it register on your thirty-nine cent plastic-made-in-Japan brain?

DORIS. Why can't we be nice to one another? We could if we tried.

FELIX. Oh God, listen to her . . . Don't you know that you're a criminal and an animal—how can I be nice to you?

DORIS. But you care for me. I know you care for me.

FELIX (shouting). That's what I'm talking about. I care for you!

DORIS. You see—you said it! You said you care for me.

FELIX. And you're so pleased by the words that choke me!

DORIS. Felix, please don't talk that way. You love me and I love you. You can't control those things. It's not your fault.

FELIX. No. Nature finds your level for you. You're right. I'm just shocked to see my level—excuse me.

DORIS. I know I'm nothing compared to you. I know that. But that doesn't mean you're like me just because you love me.

FELIX. It doesn't? Are you sure it doesn't? Doesn't your instinct tell you I'm your equal—the mate for you? Of course it tells you that!

DORIS. Oh, baby—not my equal. I'm nothing compared to you.

FELIX. Nothings can only be loved by other things. It's axiomatic.

DORIS. Don't say that. Maybe it isn't love . . . You could just be sorry for me—or maybe you love me the way you love a pet.

FELIX. There's a thought!

DORIS. Why not? A pet doesn't have any brains—you don't

have anything in common with it—but you love it, don't you?

FELIX. Is that what you want to be—my pet?

DORIS. Now don't start twisting everything.

FELIX. No, no, that sounds good—you could be my pet whore.

DORIS. Felix . . .

FELIX. Would you sleep in a box in the corner? Would you wear a collar? Would you run around the neighborhood nights? Yes, you probably would. Well, I could have you spayed, couldn't I?

(DORIS *sits looking at him helplessly.*)

Well?

DORIS. Well, what?

FELIX. I don't feel any reaction from you, how about it?

DORIS. Don't do that, Felix.

FELIX. It was your idea. Don't you even want to give it a chance? You could do it. I think you could. You're already housebroken. I'm sure you could learn a few simple tricks. Going to the market, cleaning the apartment. Give it a try. What have you got to lose? Doris . . . try it.

(*Calling a dog.*) Here Doris, here girl. (*Whistles.*) Come on Doris, come on, good girl, Doris—pretty Doris.

(DORIS *starts to cry quietly.*)

Damn it, I'm serious about this, you stupid bitch. Don't stand there like a human being!

DORIS. I don't understand what you want me to do. If you could explain it to me, I know I'd feel better.

FELIX. I want you to be a nice girl and give me your paw. Come on, give daddy your paw.

DORIS. Don't forget—I assimilated "impeccable."

FELIX. If you don't give me your paw I'm going to give you away. Now give me your paw—come on.

DORIS. You're scaring me. Why do you want to do that?

FELIX. Do you want me to give you away? Well, do you? Answer me! Do you want me to give you to some poor family who'll beat you? Answer me—

(*She shakes her head.*)

Is that so hard to do?— Is that such a difficult trick for a full-grown dog? Answer me—can't you tell me—is it hard to do?

(DORIS *shakes her head.*)

Well, then, why won't you do it?

DORIS. If I do will you stop acting like this?

FELIX. We make no deals with pets here! Give me your paw, God damn it.

(DORIS *looks at him in helpless surrender. Slowly she raises her right hand and puts it into* FELIX's *hand. He looks at her for a moment, then he melts. He bends and kisses her hand.*)

I'm sorry—I'm so sorry, Doris. Doris, please forgive me.

DORIS. It's okay. I just get a little scared, that's all. It's okay. I'd get used to it. Listen, Felix—you'd never have to even talk to me. If you felt like going out, you could just get up and walk out without even saying good-by. I wouldn't even say anything . . . Like if you said to me when we got up—"Doris, no talking today," I wouldn't even open my mouth.

(*She stops.* FELIX *looks at her.*)

Felix—

FELIX. You're very sweet.

DORIS. And another thing—

FELIX. Wait . . . Let me think for a moment.

DORIS. It's about that thinking. If it keeps hanging you up like this, maybe it isn't good for you.

FELIX. No, you're right. It's obsolete. The world has long since given it up—and here I stand, a foolish, lonely anachronism—the last of the dodo birds.

DORIS. Felix—you stop that.

FELIX. Listen to me. I'm going to be very calm and quiet and I want you to try to understand me—all right?

DORIS. Don't use any big words.

FELIX. I won't. Now listen—although you can't possibly see the reason for it—you must take my word—there's only one thing for me to do now. I've got to kill myself.

DORIS. Oh don't talk that way. You kidding?

FELIX. I'm very serious.

DORIS. But why? Why?

FELIX. Didn't I just say you can't possibly understand why?

DORIS. But sweetheart—listen—

FELIX (*interrupting*). Didn't I say that?

DORIS. Yes—

FELIX. Didn't I ask you to take my word for it? Can't you do that much for me?

DORIS. But I don't—Felix, I—(*frustrated*). Oh I could just kill you, sometimes!

FELIX (*sits at typewriter—puts in paper*). Just love me as you do, mindlessly, and see that this suicide note doesn't get lost. (*Thinking.*) . . . "To Whom It May Concern" . . .

DORIS. Oh, Felix—I don't want to live without you! I'll never find anybody else like you.

FELIX. You'll settle for less. (*Thinking.*) "To Whom It May Concern—but never does—"

DORIS. I'll never be happy. I know I won't. Didn't I try to get along without you? Why do you think I came back?

FELIX. It was only a week—

DORIS. It wouldn't make any difference how long it was. I know. I could see what kind of a life I would have. I couldn't stand it. Not now. Before I met you I could have stood it—

FELIX. Will you please shut up—I'm trying to work.

DORIS. Then just tell me—can I commit suicide with you?

FELIX. No, you can't.

DORIS. Please, Felix—why not?

FELIX. Because—I'm doing it alone—

DORIS. Will it hurt if I do it with you?

FELIX. Yes.

DORIS. Why?

FELIX. Because with me it's an affirmation of principle—a rebuke to the world—with you it would just be "monkey see, monkey do!"

DORIS. No, it wouldn't. I would be doing it for the same reason you would.

FELIX. Yours would dilute mine.

DORIS. It would not!

FELIX. How can I make her understand? Yours would be meaningless—you don't have a good reason.

DORIS. I can't live without you.

FELIX. That's a silly, sentimental suicide—that's just weakness and failure.

DORIS. And what about yours?

FELIX. Mine will be a proud, taunting, challenging suicide—a thought-provoking suicide.

DORIS. Who'll know the difference?

FELIX. My note will explain the difference. (*Thinking*.) Because truth is dead. (*Starting to type*.) Because moral courage is dead—I, Felix Sherman, choose to die—(*weighing it*) have chosen to die—

DORIS. Why can't I, Doris Wheeler, have chosen to die also?

FELIX. Doris, will you please shut up?

DORIS. You're making me real sore now. If I want to commit suicide you can't stop me—it's a free country!

FELIX (*very reasonably*). That's true! I only ask that you don't louse up mine!

DORIS. But I don't want to do it alone. I want to do it with you.

FELIX. Well, you can't and that's all there is to it.

DORIS. You're nothing but a mean selfish son of a bitch. (*She sits—angry*.) I'll fix you— I'll tear up your suicide note.

FELIX. You couldn't do a thing like that.

[117]

DORIS. I will unless you let me do it with you.

FELIX. You couldn't be so heartless.

DORIS. Look who's talking about heartless. You want to leave me all alone, don't you—you'd do that to me, wouldn't you—you don't care about me at all! Nobody does.

FELIX (*relenting*). Doris—darling—listen—

DORIS. It feels like a hot shower when you call me darling.

FELIX. My dear strange child—please try to understand why I have to do this alone—I want it to have a certain impact. I want to hit out through every morning newspaper at all—

DORIS (*interrupting*). You're very foolish from a newspaper standpoint.

FELIX. I'm trying to force the public to think about—(*Stops.*) What did you say? The newspaper standpoint?

DORIS. Certainly. What's one fellow committing suicide? You can find that in the paper any day—in the back pages—but a good suicide pact is front page news—

FELIX (*impressed with this. Then, discarding it*). Oh—but it's so cheap it's—

DORIS. Cheap? Listen, what about that beautiful note you're

writing? You want that mentioned on page thirty-two? "There was a piece of paper with writing on it on the jerk's body"—or you want it on the front page—"The dead lovers were both clutching a brilliant suicide note which said"—and so forth—

FELIX. "Nos morituri te salutamus." I think you're right.

DORIS. What is that?

FELIX. "We who are about to die, salute you." Latin.

DORIS. Oh, Felix really—"we"? Oh, honey, thank you!

FELIX (*at the typewriter*). To Whom It May Concern—we who are about to die, salute you. Good, Doris—you're right!—you're instinctively right!

DORIS. I guess it's the actress in me. How are we going to do it?

FELIX. Do what?—oh—I don't know.

DORIS. Sleeping pills are the nicest, but they're hard to get.

FELIX. Sweetheart—please let me concentrate—

DORIS. Well, I could be handling the details if you'll just give me a minute to make a decision—

FELIX. Shhh— (*Writing.*) Because truth is dead—

[119]

DORIS. I can't decide this all by myself—

FELIX (*rises and paces*). It needs a finish—

DORIS. Why don't you knock off five minutes and we'll work this out—

FELIX. Work what out?

DORIS. Then I could be making the arrangements.

FELIX. Arrangements?

DORIS. My absent-minded professor— How are we gonna do it? —gun—knife?

FELIX. Oh no!

DORIS. I couldn't agree with you more . . . But what then: We could never get enough sleeping pills.

FELIX. No—not sleeping pills. Sleeping pills have such a neurotic connotation.

DORIS. Well, we can't get them anyway . . . What else is nice and painless and—hey—right under our noses— (*Points to the stove.*)

FELIX. Gas? No—

DORIS. Why not?

FELIX. Gas is negative. Gas is passive defeat.

DORIS. Well, I give up. What do you suggest?

FELIX. Hemlock is what we need!

DORIS. Hemlock?

FELIX. That would be perfect. It would be eloquent!

DORIS. Hang ourselves from a hemlock tree?

FELIX. Hang ourselves? Oh no—hemlock is the poison of Socrates.

DORIS. Poison? I'm sorry—no sir! Not me!

FELIX. What's your objection to poison?

DORIS. Because I don't wanna burn up my insides and have cramps and like that—

FELIX. You can get painless poisons.

DORIS. Where—at the drugstore?

FELIX. Yes, as a matter of fact. You can buy poison to exterminate pests, can't you?

DORIS (*laughing*). I can just see us sitting here spraying each other with bug bombs.

FELIX. This is no joke, Doris.

DORIS. I'm sorry—but what do we say? "Pardon me, sir—we want to kill some rats, but we don't want to hurt them. They're so cute?" Now listen to Doris—Gas!

FELIX. All right—I suppose it is the only sensible way—

DORIS. Of course, dopey! And you were gonna do this alone!

FELIX. I'll finish the note.

DORIS (*going to the stove*). Now how will we work this?

FELIX (*getting a thought*). How does this sound—

DORIS. Honey, we got problems—

FELIX. What?

DORIS. Only one burner works. That's not much gas.

FELIX. It will work. We'll have to plug up the door. It will take time—

DORIS. We can't do that—let this whole big room fill up with gas?

FELIX. Why not?

DORIS. We can't waste all that gas!

[122]

FELIX. Damn it! If you're not serious about this, Doris—

DORIS. Sure I'm serious about it.

FELIX. "Waste all that gas?"

DORIS. I'm sorry—it's the way I was brought up—I can't help it.

FELIX. Well, we can't do it anyway, not really.

DORIS. What do you mean?

FELIX. Too many chinks in those old windows—too much of a draft in here—the only way gas will work in this thing is to stick your head in the oven.

DORIS. I don't think it's big enough.

FELIX. Yes it is.

DORIS. Not for both of us.

FELIX. No, but we could take turns.

DORIS. Oh yeah? No thank you. We're doing it together. "Two-gether"—not "one-gether."

FELIX. But what's the difference? I'd let you go first, naturally.

[123]

DORIS. Thanks a lot! And then you change your mind and I'm dead all by myself! . . . No thank you!

FELIX. All right. I'll go first.

DORIS. And I'm gonna sit here waiting and check you to see if you're done! . . . Forget it!

FELIX. Well, maybe we can do it together. Let's see—

(*They get down on their knees and try to fit their heads into the oven. There are ad lib "wait," "here," "now," "no, no, sideways," "look out for my nose," etc. They exhaust every possible combination of positions.* DORIS *starts to giggle.*)

FELIX (*deeply hurt*). Doris, why don't you just go home and forget all about it.

DORIS. I'm sorry, honey. It just struck me funny!

FELIX. You'd think you were playing some kind of a birthday party game. We're committing suicide, God damn it!

DORIS. I know it, Felix—I'm sorry I laughed.

FELIX. Are you sincere about this? Now really—if you're not—

DORIS. Of course I am.

FELIX. Are you sure? I hope you are.

DORIS. I am, honey. I just wanna make sure we go together—
that's all—wouldn't that be best?

FELIX. I suppose so. (*Stops.*) Wait a minute—oh—that's it! Of
course!

DORIS. What?

FELIX. It combines painlessness and dramatic impact.

DORIS. What, what?

FELIX. A jump—hand in hand from a public building—

DORIS. I don't know—a jump?

FELIX. It's perfect! Talk about news value—talk about the
front page—

DORIS. It sounds kind of scary!

FELIX. Why?— An exhilarating flight through space and then
oblivion.

DORIS. Well, I guess you wouldn't feel anything. (*Puts her
hand between her knees.*) Except a very cold breeze.

FELIX. What a gesture—what a stage setting for my note.

DORIS. What building though? This one isn't high enough—

FELIX. No—not this kind of a building—an office building. One of man's monuments to his false gods—one located in the center of town.

DORIS. We couldn't get into an office building at this hour, could we?

FELIX. No—you're right—a hotel—that's it! A hotel!

DORIS. Yeah—we could check into a room on the top floor— Oh—I've got it—I've got it! Perfect.

FELIX. What?

DORIS. The Top of the Mark. You know the bar—The Top of the Mark.

FELIX. Yes, of course. Look—a couple strolls in at the height of the evening's revelry. Quietly they ask for a table at the window—twenty floors above the shining city. They sit for a moment—perhaps they order a drink—the man takes an envelope from his pocket and props it against his glass. Then they rise. They turn to the noisy, laughing room. In a loud voice the man calls out—"Good-by Gomorrah!"

DORIS. Do I say anything?

FELIX. What? You don't say anything.

DORIS. It was my idea you know.

FELIX. All right—okay—you say something too—and then—

DORIS. What do I say?

FELIX. Whatever you want to—

DORIS. Could I say what you said "Good-by Tomorrow"?

FELIX. Good-by Gomorrah.

DORIS. What does that mean?

FELIX. Don't you remember Sodom and Gomorrah from the Bible?

DORIS. Oh yes—the two wicked cities—sure—I get it. That's good. Hey—how about "Farewell cruel world."

FELIX. Shut up.

DORIS. Why?

FELIX. Just shut up. Then together we yell—"Good-by Gomorrah" and before their horrified eyes we turn to the window —and hand in hand we jump—

DORIS. We ought to kiss first and blow kisses to the whole room. You know—good-by kisses. (*Pauses.*) You know the trouble with you? You only like your own ideas.

(FELIX *gives her a disgusted look.*)

[127]

FELIX. You just don't understand this—you don't get the values involved. It's useless! I can't work with you.

DORIS (*interrupting*). Okay—okay—don't lecture me—we'll do it your way.

FELIX. Now let me finish this note.

DORIS (*sudden thought*). Oh my God!

FELIX. What is it?

DORIS. Felix—the Top of the Mark is out.

FELIX. What?

DORIS. We can't do it from the Top of the Mark.

FELIX. Why not?

DORIS. They won't allow ladies wearing slacks.

FELIX. You're not wearing slacks.

DORIS. No, I have to go home and change to slacks before we jump.

FELIX. Change to slacks—why?

DORIS. Because I loaned my imported French panties to my

friend Anne for a date and all my others are at the laundry except one pair with holes in them and I am not jumping twenty stories in a skirt with ratty panties on.

FELIX. I don't believe my ears! I just don't believe you said that!

DORIS. Now don't panic.

FELIX. Now, wait a minute! Are you actually concerned about your panties?

DORIS. Not if I can jump in slacks, I'm not. In a skirt, yes—absolutely.

FELIX. It's too much—I can't bear it.

DORIS. Felix, will you calm down—we'll figure out another way.

FELIX. What's the use—I should have known you'd wreck it. I think I knew it all along.

DORIS. Oh, you're so stubborn! That's all. You got your heart set on the Top of the Mark. (*Sighs.*) Okay—I'll see if I can reach Anne and get my panties back. (*She dials.*)

FELIX. I should have done it alone. (FELIX *sits looking at Doris in mute despair.*)

DORIS. Hello, Janice? This is Doris—listen, it's very urgent that

I contact Anne. Have you any idea where she went with her date? Well, will you—ask Patty? (*Covers mouthpiece and addresses* FELIX.) I'd borrow a pair from her, but she buys her lingerie at Woolworth's—she's a communist or . . . Hello?—yeah? You're kidding! You sure? Thanks, Janice. (*She hangs up.*) You'll never guess in a million years where Anne is right now with her date—in my panties—

FELIX (*lifelessly*). The Top of the Mark.

DORIS. How did you know? Is that fantastic? Is that fate! Now here's what we'll do—I'll run home and change into a skirt —meanwhile you can change your shirt and put on a tie— why don't you put on your blue suit and that silver tie —then we'll go up to the Mark and we'll find Anne and her date, I'll take Anne to the ladies' room and get my panties from her— Gee, what'll I tell her why I want them? I'll just say it's my first date with you and I wanna make a good impression—meanwhile you could be—

(*She stops—*FELIX *has quietly started to tear up the suicide note.*)

What are you doing?

(FELIX *turns away from her. She goes to him.*)

FELIX. Go away.

DORIS. What's wrong?

[130]

FELIX. Nothing. You destroyed my life—why not my death? It's symmetrical.

DORIS. Is it off? Sweetheart—just tell me—I don't understand. I just wanted to help you.

FELIX (*shouting*). Will you get out of here? Get out of my sight.

DORIS (*picking up the coffee jar*). You're out of coffee. (*She puts on her coat.*) I'll be right back.

FELIX. Where are you going?

DORIS. To get some coffee.

FELIX. Not now.

DORIS. It'll just take a minute. You need a hot cup of coffee.

FELIX (*a touch of panic*). No—don't leave! Don't leave me.

DORIS. Okay—take it easy, baby—don't be afraid. (*She sits and puts her arms around him.*)

FELIX. Doris, what am I going to do?

DORIS. You know something I just realized?

FELIX. What?

DORIS. You're as bad as I am—you're scared of everything you don't understand.

FELIX (*looking heavenward*). When? When are you going to let me out? (*Listens.*) Uh-huh.

DORIS. What'd He say?

FELIX. Don't call us, we'll call you.

DORIS (*laughing*). You big dope.

FELIX. No, the word for me is failure—rat fink failure.

DORIS. We're not licked yet. We'll try again after dinner.

FELIX. Forget it, honey—it's no use.

DORIS. Listen, don't feel bad. If I hadn't been here you'd be in the papers by now—I loused you up. It was just me and my silly panties. But you can do anything, Felix, anything you want to do.

FELIX. No—no—don't feed me that. I can't live on that—wait. Wait—I wonder if—I bet that's it.

DORIS. What, Felix?

FELIX. Now listen, pay attention. My name is Fred Sherman. I'm a clerk in a bookstore. I have a pocketful of talent, but it's counterfeit. Now who are you?

DORIS. You're nuts.

FELIX. Who are you?

DORIS. Doris Wheeler.

FELIX. The model?

DORIS. And actress.

FELIX. Like hell you are! No, sir! Now, who are you?

DORIS. Why are we doing this?

FELIX. Who are you?

DORIS. I don't understand.

FELIX. Never mind. Now, who are you? Take your time. Who are you really? Don't be afraid.

DORIS. Doris Wilgus?

FELIX. Very good. And what do you do? Easy now.

DORIS. I'm a receptionist. I was formerly a prostitute—but also I was in two television commercials—

FELIX (*holding out his hand—smiling*). I thought you looked familiar. How do you do?

DORIS (*taking his hand*). Very nice meeting you, Fred. Actually it was only one commercial.

(*They hold hands lightly.*)

Curtain falls